The
LEANING
A NOVELLA
TOWER

CHARLES MCNEILL

ISBN: 978-1-960146-02-1 (hard cover)
       978-1-960146-03-8 (soft cover)

Edited by: Amy Ashby

Published by Warren Publishing
Charlotte, NC
www.warrenpublishing.net
Printed in the United States

To True Academic Freedom!

PREFACE

MOST SCHOLARS ARE PRIVILEGED to work largely within the confines of their academic towers—ivory, brick, or cement. These settings provide them with financial, social, and technological resources required to ply their trade. On the one hand, this ensures their ongoing support, relative isolation, security, and freedom to explore the world around them without interruption; on the other, such settings separate them from the "real world," making their experiences of reality indirect and limited at best, encouraging them to view reality from the inside out, subject to projections of their secluded egos onto the universe surrounding them. Their relative unawareness of such limitations is worst of all, resulting in blind debates regarding the true nature of the universe they are attempting to understand.

This novella attempts to dramatize these ideological dynamics in a completely fictional account of the behavior of academics in one department in a public university. The work to follow documents the observations and experiences of a professor and friend as they struggle to understand and endure the rituals of their colleagues in an isolated college bureaucracy. Major types of groups or networks are delineated, the activities they experience, and the destructive consequences eventually flowing from them. The protagonist, Alistair, and his friend Alex pursue their individual journeys through this pedantic swamp, attempting to maintain their sanity in the face of constant distortion, surrounded by fellow travelers largely blind to their own limitations and those of the system to which they are so powerfully bound. The tale to follow is inevitably limited in time, scope, and detail, designed primarily to illustrate some of the major traits of such contexts. The work is intended to be illustrative and insightful rather than exhaustive.

The author acknowledges and thanks both friends and editors who offered very useful suggestions regarding the manuscript. Their help is greatly appreciated.

CONTENTS

THE MAIN PLAYERS
(In Order of Appearance)

- **ALISTAIR FAIRBAIRN:** Protagonist, agonized observer, and Critic;

- **JOHN ESPOSITO:** Department chair 1971–1975, perpetual approval seeker;

- **ANDREA STARK:** Chair's unhappy administrative assistant;

- **ALEX KATZ:** Alistair's friend, comrade in arms, and Critic;

- **ALLEN PATERSON:** Department Radical, constantly demanding more resources;

- **NANCY PIERS:** Department Radical and feminist, no social filter, talks endlessly;

- **SYBIL PATTERSON:** Department Radical and feminist, dysfunctional family, becomes terminally ill;

- **ARNOLD GARLAND:** Department Insider, presumptuous self-appointed department leader, later interim chair;

- **ANDREW HUTTON:** Department Insider, number cruncher, seeks chair position;

- **MAX CRAMER:** Department Insider, popular socially, tragic early death;

- **DAVID COLES:** 1960's department chair, constant Supporter of department welfare;

- **SPENCER PARKER:** Department Supporter (later Administrator), population expert;

- **MIKE BODEN:** Marginal department hippie, rejected by colleagues, leaves to go farming;

- **JAMES FOULDS:** Vulnerable department one-term chair, authoritarian, unpopular;

- **ROY JACKSON:** Vulnerable new hire, family sociologist, popular socially, not tenured;

- **ALLISON DAVIES:** Vulnerable new hire, department's first African-American hire, not tenured;

- **ROBERT HALSTEAD:** Obnoxious demographer, highly successful, leaves department;

- **RAY MEYER:** Obnoxious demographer, highly critical of department, leaves department;

- **JAMES GRISWOLD:** Department's most Arrogant, aloof and distant, leaves department;

- **IAN EVANS:** Leader of the Mafia, hired as chair, highly manipulative, becomes terminally ill;

- **RON COVENTRY:** Administrator, college dean, conforms to donor and presidential wishes;

- **WALTER JEFFERIES:** Administrator, ineffective university president, conforms to public fads;

- **CHRISTOPHER JONES:** Earlier dean.

PART ONE: THE ACTORS

THE FALL OF 1971 HAD ARRIVED, accompanied by cool and sometimes foggy mornings. It was still relatively early, and the Ocala State campus was quiet, with a few students scuttling to the union cafeteria for their dawn fix of caffeine. Alistair walked toward the building, which appeared as gray and unwelcoming as the dawn. He paused to watch the busy squirrels for a moment, then entered. The Hambrook Social Science Building had all the appearance of an obsolescent computer card: it was tall, fairly narrow, and had thin, narrow windows rather like the personalities of its occupants, through which they could take narrow looks at an extremely narrow world. "Shambrook" had no architectural or social ambience whatsoever.

Inside, the air was heavy, the atmosphere like a mausoleum. Three automatic drink and coffee machines guarded the elevators' doorways, as though protective of their incompetent technological relatives. Alistair waited, his briefcase by his side, wondering what forces of fate could possibly have swept him from his home in Scotland to this isolated backwater in which both natives and migrants merged in a mentality of moribund mediocrity, striving to protect their fragile egos and academic ambitions.

After much clicking and squeaking, a rather weary elevator clattered open, and he stepped in. As it slowly ground its way upward, he waited, head down, for his arrival on the fourth floor where the sociology department, presently enshrouded in a gloom of lethargy, was slowly awakening to a new day. He knew the only life he could expect, apart from the obsessive chair who always arrived a full hour ahead of him, was the activity of the secretaries who would be preening themselves and brewing coffee—the addictive life-blood of the faculty who stumbled in later.

The elevator deposited him in front of the department display, in which the remains of yellowing editions of books and academic papers of yesteryear were presented in random disarray. Some had been pilfered by quick-witted students who realized the texts were not worth buying but might be needed later as class props to reinforce the worn remnants of vulnerable faculty egos. He crept past the main office, which had all the appearances of a hospital duty desk.

The inner sanctum contained John Esposito, the overly sincere department chair. He was an earnest, clean-shaven, neatly dressed person whose desire for approval was so overwhelming, it was painfully obvious. He puffed slowly on a clean pipe—ash or tobacco were never visible—and walked slowly around the department corridors, sampling colleague sentiment and approval. His face, craggy-looking but clean, reflected the joy of a shepherd who feels he knows each of his flock by name and knows they truly *need* him. He came from an immigrant background; his father had built himself up from an unskilled laborer to a skilled tradesman in the construction industry with union help. This experience of the "industrial brotherhood" left an indelible impression on John, whose greatest fear was having to make any decision independent of colleague consensus.

Consequently, faculty meetings were held almost weekly, in which John presided over a regular orgy of self-serving machinations, during which the "professors" assumed they were discussing the department's pressing financial and academic issues, when they were actually projecting their subjective fantasies onto what they perceived as threatening their psychological security.

Such gatherings were rather like vaudeville shows with teams of actors performing their routines until the anxiety of those in the wings drowned each out in turn. Alistair, while supporting democracy, saw little point in constant meetings called to vote on every conceivable issue.

Ironically, John sometimes found it difficult to keep up with each change on the program—he was easily confused—but as the show's "MC," he managed to keep it moving. He then assumed, by each meeting's conclusion, that somehow a meaningful decision had been reached under his expert guidance, at which point, he glowed with self-satisfaction. On one memorable occasion, however, he became so confused by the endless positing of alternative policy options, he cried out, "My mind has turned to jelly—let someone else here decide!" He also had an ambitious, manipulative, status-conscious wife who accorded him few options; he was a little afraid of her, with good reason.

Andrea, the head secretary, heavily preoccupied, was concentrating on her paperwork. She was a short and ill-tempered Southerner with an unhappy, and somewhat tumultuous, marriage to an air force officer, which changed the color of her complexion from time to time, making her punitive toward the predominantly male faculty. John, her confidant, listened quietly, in priest-like fashion, to her sobbing tales of domestic conflict. While this was an act he was somewhat uncertain how to "manage" since his wife never cried unless he spilled ash on the lounge carpet, he felt warm and pleased that Andrea sought his comfort and advice. In reality, he had little of the latter to offer but patted her on the shoulder as best he could and enjoyed another glow of approval. He was needed by her *also*. She appriated him, too, and tried to cater to his every whim.

Alistair scuttled down the hallway to his office just beyond the department's dingy meeting room and closed the door behind him. The offices of his colleagues were arranged in a square around the building floor. They rather reminded him of dog kennels from which the yapping of their occupants, on the rare occasions they showed up, could be heard, some much louder than others. Unfortunately, unlike sled dogs, they refused to "mush" or cooperate on any particular issue, whining instead and pulling in opposite directions. Their often-closed doors were decorated with faded copies of cartoons, and comments regarding current issues. The faculty fell into a number of distinct groups.

THE MAIN PLAYERS
The Critics

ALISTAIR HAD BEEN IN THE department for almost thirty years. He felt he had been washed up into a lagoon, attempting to return to the ocean without success. High school, college, and graduate school achievements had come easily to him since he was always motivated to be highly productive. His professional accomplishments included numerous published books and research papers. Whining, stupidity, or academic politics only annoyed him since they stood in the way of a creative environment. He had a very pragmatic mentality based on his Scottish background, favoring practical action over talk, with as little delay as possible.

Alex Katz and he had become close friends from the start, partly due to their mutual cynicism regarding the university and department. He had been in the department even longer than Alistair. They thought of themselves as aging observers in an upstairs balcony, rather like seniors watching the usual department vaudeville show below, cackling and deriding those onstage for acting out their predictable routines. Alex also had a biting tongue, once emphasizing in a meeting that his colleagues were apparently unaware their antics were the "laughingstock" of the whole college. The two of them even invented a language, in which they parodied everyday conversation by reducing it to the most banal, predictable, vacuous expressions. When they wanted to avoid meaningful discussion, they drowned out those they spoke to with these phrases, keeping everyone at a significant distance, while others thought they were actually engaged in meaningful conversation. They used it with each other and strangers, adding new words and expressions constantly with extreme enjoyment and hilarity. This acted as a secret dialect that appeared completely normal to the uninitiated.

When summer arrived, for example, Alistair couldn't resist jumping in:

"Looks like it's going to be another scorcher!" he said to Alex.

"You've got that right, but it's not the heat, it's the humidity!" Alex exclaimed.

"I suppose we will get our usual daily storm," said Alistair.

"That's one bad thing about living in Florida—that and the hurricanes," responded Alex.

"That's the price you pay for warm winters," explained Alistair.

"It certainly costs you enough in electricity," concluded Alex.

"Yes, but I couldn't stand those northern winters," commented Alistair.

And so it continued. Where would it all end? The foundation for later action had been laid.

Next came the agitators.

The Radicals

THIS FACTION CONSTANTLY ARGUED to support the more deprived in society, particularly themselves. They strongly supported unionization, along with greater financial resources to assist both faculty and students. They felt they were representing the downtrodden subject to major forms of inequality in society at large. Their refrain was always predictable: They were on a *mission*! They wanted to *save* the powerless; however, they were largely concerned with obtaining control for themselves rather than others or the department as a whole—they wanted primarily to advance their own interests and fulfill their specific resource needs. To accomplish this, they wanted to make resources and opportunities more readily available for everyone in the department but particularly themselves. Their leader was Allen Paterson.

Allen sat at the front of the department's conference room located next to Alistair's office, staring out the window. A self-appointed Radical who lived in a plush, comfortable home and owned a large boat and new car, he always arrived well-groomed. Like John, he was a union supporter and had agitated constantly for unionization of the faculty and graduate students, seeking collective bargaining with the administration on every possible issue. In his classes and discussions with colleagues, he constantly highlighted his own research, feeling his insight was vital to all concerned. A friend had jokingly referred to Allen as an "elephant who thought he was a cheetah." The image stuck for years. The pachyderm eventually retired in early 1990 and left town permanently. Once, a student told Alistair that Paterson had made her feel so guilty about the poor in society, she felt so nauseated and could barely bring herself to eat dinner when she arrived home.

Nancy Piers also showed up regularly—to the dismay of her colleagues, she came in almost every day. Her mind had no social filter at all; whatever came into her brain was immediately verbalized, often very loudly and, occasionally, inappropriately. Once, a student had asked Alistair where her office was located. Alistair simply held his hand up to the student's ear and said, "Just listen." Alex was standing next to him at the time and was unable to restrain his laughter.

She was largely into number crunching, particularly social survey data, and primarily enjoyed teaching research methods. Her students found her dynamic to a fault, sometimes unable to follow her erratic train of thought. Her enthusiasm, however, was unmistakable, and she was driven to share her ideas and research with all in earshot. Toward the end of 1999, her annual evaluations would become problematic, and she would later transfer to a different college.

Sybil Paterson was Nancy's colleague—a quieter and more occasional visitor. She, like Nancy, was supportive of gender equality and related issues in a male-dominated department but much calmer in her reactions. Ironically, her major specialty was family sociology, despite her own domestic situation being close to total meltdown. Ignoring these domestic distractions, she labored on and continued to be appreciated by her students, both undergraduate and graduate.

Interestingly, some years back, Alistair had developed the "Law of Opposites" as applied to academics: economists did not manage their money well, many marriage counselors were divorced, some counselors clearly had mental problems of their own, and sociologists were unmistakably socially inept! This principle was constantly illustrated at Ocala; faculty in all areas demonstrated their inadequacies in their personal and professional lives—the latter in particular—inhibiting significant social change.

Like Nancy, Sybil felt strongly about women's rights, energetically supporting gender studies and faculty equality in the department and university at large. Given her personal and career frustrations, however, she had become increasingly outspoken and harshly strident concerning academic policies and programs. Her personal life became further complicated and conflict-ridden when she proceeded with a very hostile divorce. In 2001, she would become ill and later pass away, assigned to the fading memory bank of the department's largely neglected history.

While agreeing with this clique in many respects, Alistair found relating to them difficult and unpleasant at times, particularly with Allen, whose self-absorption was hard to tolerate. The constant refrain, "What have you done for me lately?" became irksome, rapidly losing its critical edge. Nevertheless, their reactions were always present, fueling Alistair's rising anger and frustration.

Even more delusional were the self-appointed elite.

The Insiders

THE NEXT THREE COLLEAGUES—Arnold, Andrew, and Max—
participated aggressively in most faculty meetings, arguing for
greater unionization of faculty and graduate students, institutional
democracy at all levels, and greater resources from the dean and
university at large. They defined themselves as the department's
true leaders, responsible for its general welfare and future direction.

Arnold Garland was one of these and led the group. He had been
at Ocala State almost as long as Alistair. His self-confidence was
very high, particularly when it came to his teaching; he constantly
aspired to instructional awards at all levels of the university. A little
older than some, he felt his life and academic experience qualified
him to be a leader and had sought this role from the start. He felt
he, along with a couple of colleagues, essentially ran things for
the other faculty and represented their welfare extremely well. His
behavior, as well as that of the rest of his trio, never ceased to amaze
Alistair, who concluded that academics in particular exhibited
constant insecurity, aggravated by their isolation from everyday
reality in the ivory—or in this case, cement—tower. The Insiders
constantly tried to convince the dean that their unit required more
of *everything*: faculty positions, higher salaries, larger budgets,
more graduate student fellowships, and in particular, greater
respect as the college's leading department.

Andrew Hutton was a second member of the Insiders. Tall and thin with a narrow mustache, he smoked constantly. He took number crunching to an even higher level than Nancy—it was all he cared about. He had previously been the recipient of large research grants and, based on these, had brought some major data files to Ocala. These contained national samples of opinion data, which he mined constantly. He had a well-developed, strong ego but, as with others, wanted to be admired and approved while remaining in control.

His previous appointments had also been bureaucratic, and this had a major effect on his behavior. On one occasion, he had loaned a few books on college student research to Alistair who kept them for some time. Wanting them returned, instead of just asking in person, Andrew wrote Alistair a formal memorandum requesting their return and sent it to him through campus mail. The latter found this incredible; he went down to his office immediately and returned the borrowed items in amazement, emphasizing that *all* Andrew had to do was ask.

Max Cramer occupied an office adjacent to his fellow Insiders. Since he was young and enthusiastic, he related to the students very well, both undergraduate and graduate. At the center of the social life of the department's in-group, he participated passionately. He had graduated from a top national program in family sociology and appeared to have a promising future. He provided major encouragement to the Insiders' partying habits, sometimes at the department and elsewhere, including local bars near campus. Unfortunately, in 1985 he met his demise; while out cutting firewood, he was crushed by a huge tree. His loss was a major blow to the department as a whole.

The Insiders politicked, socialized, drank, and partied together. They also collectively prepared for faculty meetings ahead of time—planning strategy, lobbying, and steering the resulting discussion. They appropriated the meeting "reins" from John as quickly as possible after his opening statement and then were "off to the races."

In contrast, the department's advocates took a more balanced approach to academic issues.

The Supporters

ON THE POSITIVE SIDE, the Supporters were highly concerned with the general welfare and ongoing development of the department as a whole. This faction was comprised of just two faculty: David and Spencer. They tried to act rationally in all departmental matters and bring moderation and pragmatism to discussion of the unit's needs, with only limited concern for their own programs.

David Coles, like Max, contributed positive energy and support to the unit. He had actually recruited and hired Alistair, supporting him through some of Alistair's more difficult periods in an occasionally hostile environment. Unlike others, he was highly committed to the long-term welfare of the department and college generally. He had established a highly successful training program in population studies and obtained a large training grant used to bring in international students from third-world countries, particularly Asia, preparing them to serve their own governments. He was chair when Alistair first arrived but stepped down shortly afterward. Both Alistair and Alex relied on him for sane advice during difficult times, always finding him calm and helpful.

Spencer Parker was also a Supporter who focused on population issues, arriving some years after Alistair, during the late 1970s. He had been recruited in the South and was expected to fit well into the training center. Alistair hosted him during his interview trip and found him pleasant, interesting, and insightful. They cooperated well. Spencer settled in easily and quickly became part of the population group. While not entirely comfortable with Halstead, he managed to keep his distance and cooperate well with the group as a whole. Later, when considered for promotion and tenure, Spencer would be attacked by the Mafia in the 1990s—arrogant members of the department who had been recruited in the 1980s. He would calmly address all their concerns and be promoted successfully. Later, he would become chair for two terms. Alistair respected and liked him; they worked well together over many years.

While a minority, this faction helped moderate the simplistic cheerleading and demands of most of their colleagues, often calming the department's unnecessarily troubled waters.

On the quieter side were the more excluded.

The Marginal and Vulnerable

A NUMBER OF DEPARTMENT MEMBERS were vulnerable to their colleagues' actions regarding committee elections, academic status, or promotion and tenure. They took "back seats" at meetings, remaining largely unnoticed. Alistair was deeply disturbed by the inhumane, inconsistent manner in which they were treated. They were often used as "ego-fodder" to reinforce their insecure colleagues' self-confidence, frequently at the cost of due process.

Back in the 1970s, Mike Boden was one of these. He rarely appeared and had essentially abandoned his position at "Redneck Tech." He spent his days drinking and drugging, holding his classes outdoors when possible, on the lawn in front of Hambrook, and was now living with one of his students. His disillusionment with academic life had begun several years back when he suddenly realized it was all an empty, competitive game. He joined the Hippie Generation, dropping out and ridiculing his colleagues for their intense participation in the college rat race, fighting endlessly over meager rewards.

Dressed in overalls, this deviant colleague presented the image of a "country bumpkin" among serious academics. On one well-remembered occasion, Boden had left a plain carton in the department's conference room before an important evaluation meeting. Someone inadvertently disturbed it, setting off a musical box inside, which played an ironic cheerleading tune. Many attendees could barely control their hilarity and embarrassment. Consequently, he attracted the anger and contempt of many of his associates who felt he should be fired immediately for not treating the "game" seriously. Due process be damned, in their opinion, he deserved to be "drummed out of the corps." Eventually, he'd make the decision to resign, advertising the books in his office as a "fired sale," and go out west in search of more practical pursuits, such as farming.

James Foulds—or "Jim," as he was known—specialized in family sociology. He was older and more traditional than his colleagues, believing strongly in family values and kinship obligations. His simplistic judgments of department faculty were resented while his sexist remarks on women bordered on the inappropriate, flattering them in ways they didn't welcome. He exemplified the type of traditional male who wanted to control everything and everyone but be admired at the same time.

During 1979, when Jim was considered for renewal as chair, most of his colleagues were offended by his personality and decision-making idiosyncrasies and selected another candidate. He was deeply hurt and outraged—how could they do this to him when he had worked so hard to help them and the department?

"What more could I have done for all of you?" he cried. "You are completely ungrateful and despicable!"

Most were greatly relieved when he later left Ocala permanently.

Roy Jackson's specialty was family sociology also. He was a junior hire who had arrived from graduate school in the early 1970s before his dissertation was complete. As such, he required some time to settle in, complete his degree, and begin to publish. In his twenties and younger than most of his colleagues, he enjoyed the students and teaching in general. He also enjoyed partying and related to his students more than to his new colleagues. He started working with Jim Foulds during the mid-1970s, and together they developed a paper that was later published by a well-known sociological journal. This resulted in a sigh of relief and the hope that he was now on his way. However, as the 1980s progressed, he managed no more than a trickle of attempts that appeared in relatively unknown publications. While Roy was quite popular in the department, his weak productivity made him vulnerable regarding possible promotion. He once confided to Alistair, "A lot of my 'supporters' were talking out of both sides of their mouths at the same time. They were snakes, as I learned later, why did I ever trust them?"

During the 1980s, the department would implement affirmative action and decide to recruit Allison Davies, sociology's first African-American professor. She was very pleasant and sincere, had completed some interesting work in her dissertation, and had also obtained a grant to support it. However, her methodological skills were not particularly strong, and she had difficulties analyzing and interpreting her data. Her teaching style was positive but not very stimulating since she lacked experience in this skill, taking a rather stiff, static approach in her delivery. She presented her lectures as a series of descriptive, rather than dynamic, statements. She continued to move ahead, however, and faced her first consideration for promotion and tenure, which did not go well. Waiting another year, she resubmitted her candidacy and was initially promoted but later voted down for tenure. Alistair was extremely concerned for her welfare and supported her as much as he could.

This group was attacked and scapegoated by many in the department. While Alistair and Alex appreciated their limitations, they found this vicious treatment of their weaker colleagues unfair and infuriating reactions that only grew over time. They were either absent or largely silent in the back rows at department meetings, apart from responding to any rare questions directed at them.

On the opposite side sat the demanding, interfering, and autocratic.

The Obnoxious and Arrogant, the Mafia Network, and Manipulative Factions

THIS CLIQUE INCLUDED THE most presumptuous, self-centered, and in some cases, manipulative faculty, entirely motivated by their own interests and those of their immediate friends. The majority had arrived in the department recently and were the most egotistical of all. They assumed they ran the show. The Obnoxious were both outspoken and demanding while the Arrogant presumed they knew best. Behind the scenes, the Manipulators did their best to have their way; ironically, they were rarely successful. Teaming up with the Insiders, they all worked together, attempting to dominate the whole scene, with the Vulnerable and Weak subject to their tyranny, and opposing Critics and Supporters trying to defend the department's welfare.

Robert Halstead, the most obnoxious, was a population expert who had joined the department in 1970. He was neither positive nor pleasant most of the time. Extremely brash, he disregarded his health entirely and smoked continuously, polluting his office and surrounding areas. He was highly successful at publishing papers in prestigious journals. Exceeding most of his colleagues in securing research and instructional grants came easily to him. Like David, the previous chair who had hired Alistair, Robert had established a well-funded graduate training program, attracting large numbers of international students from a number of parts of the world and preparing them for crucial government service. No promotion or tenure criteria could slow him down, and he quickly became a full professor. His contempt for many of his colleagues, however, ensured he remained a social and academic isolate. During the late 1980s, he became editor of a major journal in his field and rapidly became well-known. At meetings, Robert always expressed *exactly* how he felt, no matter how caustic or critical he was of his colleagues. While Alistair enjoyed his acidic sense of humor, he avoided working with him, not wanting to become one of his targets.

Ray Meyer, another demographer, was also unpleasant but less so than Robert. He was very research-oriented and had little enthusiasm for students or attempting to teach them. Several of his annual evaluations highlighted this deficiency, and he was forced to submit himself to remedial teaching workshops. He was also successful at obtaining research grants and was part of the graduate training program. He defined himself primarily as a research scientist, and minimized his teaching obligations as much as possible before eventually finding a full-time research position elsewhere.

In forthcoming decades, during which he participated in future shows, James Griswold would later join the department as its most arrogant member. He would transfer to Ocala State during the 1990s from a more prestigious university to facilitate his younger wife's career. He felt he was not only a sociologist but also a social philosopher—the department's only true intellectual. He soon published a multivolume work on the sociology of knowledge most readers found obtuse and confusing. Jim felt his extensive background in philosophy and the social sciences placed him well ahead of his colleagues at the academy. What did they know about the history and foundation of "knowledge"? He was highly critical of most graduate students, feeling they lacked adequate academic backgrounds and reading skills.

He arranged small conferences of like-minded academics who flew in for their seminars, in which their Insider language and shared academic interests reigned. In these sessions, James appeared to feel his theoretical ideas were "pushing the envelope" and have a significant impact on society generally—*fat chance*!

Another later-arrival in the 1990s would include Ian Evans, a close colleague of James's, known to those outside his network as the "Great Manipulator." He would likewise migrate from a more prestigious university to Ocala, in his case, to achieve promotion and assume the chair role in 1982. He applied great pressure to bring his friends with him, ensuring they won the game of a national search, in which the outcome was already guaranteed. His interaction with colleagues was always uncomfortable as he desperately manipulated to get his way in most matters. He tried to cajole and wheedle faculty into accomplishing his goals for him. Many could feel his motives were kept hidden as he attempted desperately to achieve his personal goals and impress the dean. Others could feel the hair on the back of their necks rising when he approached. He was also known as the "snake" to some who clearly saw through his crude antics and political moves; they found him despicable and never to be taken at face value. Whenever he approached, you knew he wanted something you probably were unwilling to provide.

Ian was determined to move the sociology department upward to fame and fortune, promoting himself in the process. He imposed great pressure on the faculty to publish in prestigious journals and obtain large research grants. Promotion and tenure among the outgroup became increasingly difficult to attain, as they were subjected to significant delay and nitpicking by Ian and other Mafia members, particularly James. On one occasion, he pressured Alistair into applying for a complicated grant that was extremely time-consuming and unsuccessful in attaining funding since he was not part of the professional sociology's inner networks. In general, Ian spent much of his time and energy attempting to guarantee the outcome of recruiting, promotion, and tenure considerations. He *always* wanted to have his way at *any* price. However, his effectiveness in transforming the department was clearly flawed, and he stepped down as chair during 1995, attempting unsuccessfully to achieve reelection later. Eventually, he'd become seriously ill and pass away. Few would grieve. Alistair would not attend the memorial.

The Administrators

IN GENERAL, THE ADMINISTRATORS ruled from a distance, choosing to intervene only when necessary and then only for selfish reasons. Little attention was ever paid to detail or infrastructure improvements, which were sorely needed. They represented cheerleading at another level; nevertheless, the Beast (i.e., Ocala State administration) always won, and mediocrity, camouflaged as mounting excellence, was maintained at all cost.

Ron Coventry would later become the college dean in 2008. He was extremely tall and thin, had some major immunity deficiencies, and was similar in appearance to a stork perched on one foot. He was greatly dependent on his female assistant, whom he admired greatly and followed around like a lost puppy. Like others, he believed the college was on an upward track to fame and fortune due to his efforts; he savored each tiny increase in rank as the decades went by, and congratulated himself for being responsible.

However, Ron had his detractors, some of whom suspected he was too subjected to the influence of external donors. He went to great lengths to demonstrate this was not the case, but serious doubts remained. In addition, he tolerated some weak chairs and programs, allowing them to limp along unhindered, engaging in financial practices that were potentially damaging to the college. He also gave in to every incoming president, praising their flawed efforts to improve the university despite their obvious defects. He always adjusted to the incoming elite, constantly playing to their desires with enthusiasm. He welcomed Alistair's help as long as it suited his interests, dumping him later when it did not. Not surprisingly, Alistair would rapidly come to despise and ridicule Ron for his willingness to compromise, viewing him as bowing to any Administrators who took office. He always courted approval from above and was always prepared to do anything to achieve it.

As the state's economic future appeared in decline, Ron would step down in 2016, handing over to one of his handpicked protégés who continued his fine tradition of illusion and mediocrity. He clearly did not want to be associated with any kind of perceived failure.

Considering Ron and the many Administrators Alistair had experienced over previous decades, the latter sat back after the dean's resignation and marveled at how academic conditions at Ocala had never varied significantly at all during the many years he had been there; only delusions and demographics changed significantly. The administration's seamless continuity never wavered whatever others attempted to modify. In fact, it was almost a source of comfort that Ocala State appeared totally immune to meaningful modification, no matter who or how much anyone tried. Administrators came and left, exhausting themselves in their attempts to impose improvements, with little perceivable impact. The Ocala Beast always survived.

Ocala had its presidents appointed by nonacademic boards who frequently imposed ex-politicians with no academic credentials whatsoever. The consequences were often embarrassing, to say the least. Politics and blindness largely ruled the day. The other part of the ritual often involved conducting a national search and then discovering that, after all, the best candidate was there all the time!

Walter Jefferies had been the university's president for several years prior to Ron's 2008 appointment. He was an ex-politician who had served in the state legislature, graduated from the university with two degrees, and was a rabid Ocala fan to the point of blindness. Faculty and students vigorously opposed his appointment; this was no qualified academic by any stretch of the imagination, and they did not approve of him, particularly his narrow beliefs. The selection committee, however—composed primarily of lawyers, business people, and politicians—overruled the opposition, and Walter was eventually offered the post.

He represented little more than a lobbyist and alumnus; nevertheless, he assumed his new position with enthusiasm and vigor. Outsourcing most academic matters to his provost, he became a roving ambassador for the university and was popular among its unthinking cheerleaders and Board of Trustees. Regarding controversial matters, he always "went with the flow"; not all appreciated such actions, however, and he looked forward to an early retirement, rapidly fading into anonymity.

Alistair viewed presidential appointments with concern and contempt; he felt the selection process sidestepped and often insulted faculty opinion with destructive results. While such "leaders" might be successful at lobbying the legislature for money and rallying community support, they worked against faculty morale as well as implementation of significant improvements. However, many Administrators and faculty quickly adjusted to their unwelcome regimes, acting in disingenuous ways to gain approval and achieve their personal goals. Blindness and irrationality reigned at Ocala's highest levels, frustrating Alistair even further.

THE REHEARSAL

EVERY ACADEMIC YEAR began with the department meeting. The shabby conference room next to Alistair's office was the permanent venue into which both the enthusiastic and reluctant shuffled. The windows permitted dim light since they had not been cleaned in years. The walls contained old photographs of previous chairs, a blackboard used for seminars, and dingy green paint, desperately requiring redecorating. The stage was set for a "rehearsal" of future "shows."

The usual obsessions included limited resources and inadequate faculty positions. The welfare and future of the department were viewed as in crisis—that was *always* the case. Faculty never felt they received enough respect, recognition, financial resources, staff, or faculty positions to meet the department's needs or, more importantly, reflect positively on them. How these issues were raised, discussed, and then addressed varied according to which faculty faction "had the floor," of course.

John Esposito, their enthusiastic chair, arrived a little late, and the "show" was on. His customary script included a summary of last year's achievements, a welcome to new faculty and graduate students—now attendees at such meetings—and committee chair reports. Each faculty group had assumed their positions in the room: Critics sitting on the sidelines near the exit; Radicals, Insiders, the Obnoxious, Arrogant, and Manipulative surrounding the chair near the table head; and the Marginal, Vulnerable, and Supporters filling the chairs along the walls. Alistair entered the room and waited for Alex to join him. Upon the latter's arrival, they waited for the event to begin.

John launched into his expected presentation of all the department's "good" news. "Our present condition appears strong, and with further resources from the dean, we should be able to climb to new heights quite easily in the near future."

As the department's Critics, Alistair and Alex remained largely on the margin, positioning themselves near the conference room's doors in case their disgust got the better of them, and they had to leave early. They only participated in the meeting in limited fashion to ask pointed questions regarding issues such as student enrollment and graduation rates, knowing this often embarrassed the chair and other colleagues whose responses were always brief, inadequate, and largely unenlightening.

Alistair asked, "What are the exact doctoral graduation rates, undergraduate and graduate enrollments, and faculty raises this past year? Has salary inversion for any faculty member been addressed recently?"

John frowned with annoyance and responded impatiently with, "I will have to research those data and get back to you, Alistair." Their constant querying irritated John, and this was reflected in his face and tone of voice.

Such reactions only reinforced Alistair and Alex's well-founded cynicism regarding the true nature of the department. Given that it was largely built on illusion, its future turned out to be unstable and shaky at best.

At department meetings, Allen, the department's major Radical, invariably demanded more for himself, the students, and the department, urging the chair to speak up more with the dean. He constantly stated, "John, I really feel we need to make more demands on the dean and facilitate unionization as soon as possible."

John always replied, "I'm doing the best I can. As for unionization, you need to take that up with the administration."

The usual nonresponse, Alistair thought of such banter.

The Radicals were among the department's most outspoken— Allen and, to a lesser extent, Nancy and Sybil. Allen had been at Ocala longer than Alistair and, given his own slow promotion, resented the latter being hired at the associate level. He emphasized that the chair should constantly be in the dean's office, demanding more resources *ad nauseum*. "Time to pressure the dean, John. We continue to deserve much greater support, given our rising quality and reputation."

While John agreed, he became weary of the constant refrain, blurting out, "I *always* do my best to represent your views on these matters."

Allen shrugged dismissively at his obvious ineffectiveness.

Nancy and Sybil were moderate feminists based on the significance of gender and their understanding of this kind of inequality in the department and American society in general. Since the overwhelming majority of their colleagues in sociology were male, their views were understandable. However, while a personal perspective is one thing, viewing every issue through the same lens becomes distorting and limiting if applied too often.

Sybil was less interested in union matters, concentrating instead on her teaching and work in family sociology. She showed some interest in theoretical issues and had discussed some of these with Alistair at one point. Both faculty brought fresh viewpoints to colleagues and students alike, adding to the department's diversity in significant ways and elaborating the students' understanding of social inequality in a variety of forms. Sibyl and Nancy were clearly self-oriented but, in a manner, not nearly as selfish as Allen.

As usual, Nancy spoke up, rambling endlessly about her research and resource needs, as she yet again sought more to support her activities. The two women persistently raised issues concerning female faculty and enrollments, financial support, course offerings on sexism, and the ongoing problem of inequality in the department.

Nancy asked, "John, when are we ever going to receive adequate funding to recruit more female faculty and students, as well as offer more courses on sexual inequality? We need far greater diversity and equity in the department if we are to reflect society generally."

John responded, "Nancy, I am doing my best, as you know, forever pressuring the dean for such increased support. While he tries sometimes, he hasn't been forthcoming on such matters in quite a while now."

Another feeble nonresponse, thought Alistair.

Less constructive were the Insiders—Arnold, Andrew, and Max. As the department's self-defined "movers and shakers," they felt they were "at the helm," guiding and ensuring the unit's future. In some ways, they did provide some positive contributions: popular teaching, national data banks, student guidance, and attempts to make internal processes more open and democratic.

Arnold, their leader, had an endless refrain that was well-known: "John, where are we on graduate assistantships, faculty lines, raising money, and the department budget?"

John responded as best he could, but it was never enough. Greater support was always demanded to ensure the department's upward trajectory. The Insiders' energy, particularly Arnold's, supported the department's academic dynamism as it grew and developed. However, their own needs were all but overwhelming; their search for approval, popularity, status, rewards, and power dominated their lives. Again, they illustrated a kind of male ambivalence—the desire for approved, camouflaged dominance.

Arnold continued by listing his demands, "We need more resources, more faculty, more money, bigger budgets, more graduate student support, and certainly more respect from the dean! After all, we are the best sociology department in the South, if not the country, and should be recognized and rewarded as such." These constant demands lost their critical edge to the point where most of the audience no longer really heard them.

David, as one of the unit's Supporters, spoke calmly, emphasizing that, "We have come quite a long way at this point, given our starting point and past limitations. What is relevant now is to build on our strengths and seek resources to move us forward even further, using well-founded evidence and supporting arguments."

Spencer, a fellow Supporter, always backed him up when needed, stressing that upward progress was always a gradual path. Unfortunately, their sage advice was largely ignored by the majority. David had a long history of constructive efforts through effective leadership, even contributing his own funds, on occasion, to enhance faculty and student efforts. More than once, the pair had assumed the chair's roles, and always took the department's needs and welfare to heart.

Next were the Obnoxious, the Arrogant, and the Manipulative, collectively known as the "Mafia." The group was exemplified by James, and later Ian and Robert. James typified the first of the group's three descriptors; distant, verbose, presumptuous, and difficult, he lived on the outer edge of the department, part of the Mafia but not visibly close to its members. He felt he was several levels above most of the locals who were undistinguished and had been around too long. He kept his ideas "close to his chest," reserving them for those in his handpicked circle of similar academics. After a couple of decades in the department, he would retire early, searching for academic rewards elsewhere.

During the early 1990s, Ian and James, known as the "academic Mafia," would circle the department like invading vultures. They were great fans of faculty citation data to the point of obsession. Alistair and Alex used to joke about installing a digital board in the department that displayed faculty citation data rather like stock quotes. Faculty could gather around daily and check their "citation stock trends."

Ironically, it was never clear if Ian was actually good friends with his ingroup colleagues. He had worked closely with them during his early Ocala days, pressuring them to meet his needs, but many of them later kept their distance. While similar to the others, he was a different type of manipulator. He had moved to Ocala specifically for promotion and to become chair; his reputation was now on the line. Consequently, he applied great pressure to the faculty to be productive in all the right places, obtain research grants, and boost the department's national ratings.

He persistently emphasized in every meeting, "We can rise to the top of the state and nation, if only we get organized and try hard enough."

All of Ian's leadership skills served these goals as he strove for personal professional prestige. The pressure was *always* on. Long discussions of strategies were held regarding changes designed to boost the department's eminence as efficiently as possible.

Many faculty pledged their loyalty and enthusiasm for such goals. But Alistair was not impressed. Nevertheless, Ian's efforts, supported by his loyalists, continued unabated, designed to impress the dean most of all. Their success, however, was extremely limited; as usual, the Beast won.

Robert was clearly the most obnoxious of all their colleagues. However, his academic and professional success, combined with his skill at obtaining research and training funding, made him largely immune to retaliation of any kind. He could "write his own ticket" for whatever he wanted. He helped support and run graduate training programs, edited major journals, and consulted with major organizations around the country. He could also be relied on to be bitingly honest in public. He felt the department had a long way to go to gain meaningful prestige and academic quality, and openly complained at many department meetings, stating, "Most of you clearly don't know what it takes to ensure a prestigious and effective department at either state or national levels." No wonder he was unpopular!

Lastly came the Marginal and Vulnerable, who largely sat in silence. In this case, Mike, as a rebel, was the major outlier. He was the target of his colleagues, labeled as one who had rejected and essentially left the "game." His contempt for their lifestyles and for offering an alternative model of a faculty lifestyle disturbed them. Roy and Allison were also exposed as weak candidates for promotion and tenure. And Jim had made a weak chair and was not reelected. At meetings, they only participated on the rare occasions they attended and were only asked occasional questions.

The rehearsal gradually stuttered to a close—its announcements, positing, demands, critical questions, and defensive nonresponses finally over. Little was actually achieved; rather, the ritual of actors preening and presenting themselves in public to stroke their insecure personal identities continued. The process was closed and self-reinforcing, an end in itself. Self-congratulation was the order of the day. And frustration was *always* guaranteed.

MUSINGS

"SOME SHOW!" COMMENTED Alistair later as he discussed the meeting with Alex in his office, his rage and frustration continuing to grow. He stopped to consider the scene as a whole: always waiting to take the stage were the Insiders, Radicals, Arrogant, Manipulators, and Obnoxious, to a lesser extent the Supporters, and the Vulnerable making rare, if any, appearances or comments. As the Critics, Alistair and Alex served as an audience, observing the "performance" from the outside, as they predicted the actors' usual routines, barely able to restrain their cynical mirth when they were on target. They knew what to expect before each performance began, with its typical overblown, bombastic portrayals of departmental achievements on all fronts, forever requiring significant resource increases to elaborate their positive halo effect!

Alistair continued, "How predictable and lame was all of that?"

Alex agreed, "About as fascinating as the daily weather report."

"What's the point, then? It is *always* the same—tiresome and vacuous."

Alex concluded, "The self-reinforcing routine *is* the point—without it, how do our colleagues know *who* they *are*?" He laughed at the irony of this but couldn't restrain his sarcasm and disgust.

Alistair agreed, "The irony is that they aren't even aware of what they're doing most of the time."

"If they were, they would probably remain in denial and continue their delusional spewing of self-serving praise."

"What is so striking is the twisted, delusional nature of academic debate in this one-sided environment. Notions of 'objectivity' and 'rationality' are entirely absent—extremely ironic given that many academics assume they are completely unbiased!"

Alex agreed completely.

Contemplating all of this, Alistair became intensely aware of the personal damage this twisted academic environment had caused him: as an outsider subject to the abusive dominance, attempted manipulation, and occasional ridicule of others, his inner rage was starting to mount, revealed in his sarcastic comments in meetings and destructive inner thoughts, particularly his plans for later revenge. In the past, he had wrongly assumed academics pursued the truth, wherever it might lead. Instead, abstract concepts and arguments, combined with subjective motives, resulted in inaccurate, invalid, and unfair judgements. *What a mess!* he thought. *What can be done about it?*

Any time he started talking about the department and university, he began to rant in anger and had to force himself back to the topic at hand. Much to his encouraging wife's and his children's dismay, he had developed obesity, high blood pressure, marginal diabetes, and gout. His family was a very significant support system in his life. He had met Heather, his wife and his childhood sweetheart, while at high school in Glasgow. She was very quiet, calm, creative, kind, empathetic, and slow to anger—essentially, Alistair's opposite. They were the perfect balance. Their two daughters, now young adults, were similar to their mother and already highly accomplished. While rather different in personality, they were both strong supporters of their parents.

While he could always rely on the department's Supporters and tried to help the Vulnerable, Alistair operated in a largely poisonous environment that continuously challenged the core of his personal values and professional integrity. Self-restraint was increasingly hard to maintain, and he feared a major explosion might be on his horizon. He had tried to exercise, meditate, and take short vacations to relieve him of the constant stress; however, these measures were largely ineffective. Nevertheless, his patient, considerate spouse was always encouraging and an important counterbalance to his rising negativity.

He emphasized his concerns to Alex, stating, "If I'm not careful enough, I will unconsciously blurt out my disgust with the department and its faculty, which would only count against me seriously."

Alex agreed, emphasizing, "You need to remember to stay camouflaged in the background. Otherwise, you will become a constant target, with the Insiders and Manipulators gunning for you."

Alistair appreciated the advice, commenting, "I know you're right, but it's mighty hard to do most of the time. The idiots surrounding you are so provocative in their biased views and behavior, that they make you go ballistic quite easily."

Similarly, Roy, the young family sociologist seeking promotion and tenure, found himself subjected to hypocrisy, inconsistency, and criticism; all of this affected him powerfully.

Both men were beginning to react strongly to this contaminated milieu. This was increasingly evident in Alistair's declining health as he smoked and drank more, and slept less. He began to experience the beginnings of heart problems and diabetes. His temper also had an increasingly short fuse. Roy experienced a similarly destructive path, drinking and partying more, in his case. While younger, his physical condition was starting to decline also as he risked similar overreaction to his colleagues. Both his body and emotions were stressed. There are *always* unavoidable consequences.

Despite their familiarity with previous "shows," Alistair and Alex remained temporarily unaware of what they were about to experience. While highly cynical, given many years of experience, they could never have anticipated their own future behavior or that of others. Offstage poised the dean with little to offer, and the president with even less. The annual meeting was over: the actors were in place; their actions were about to follow the rehearsal.

PART TWO: THE ACTION

THE FALL OF 1972 ARRIVED after a rather uneventful year had passed. After months of heat, humidity, and vital air conditioning, the weather was finally tolerable, if not enjoyable at times. Ocala's campus was filled with returning and new students moving enthusiastically into their new accommodations, starting their classes, and eagerly anticipating football games and partying—their major priorities. For faculty, the summer always provided a relief from constant teaching, meetings, and academic politics. Returning refreshed, some of them had been reenergized for the battles ahead. Others, more fatigued, dragged themselves back for more of the same, though hoping desperately for better.

It never came.

Alistair's relaxing summer had offered him time to recover from recent events and refuel for the new year. He particularly benefitted from reduced teaching obligations, lack of meetings, and distance from his annoying colleagues. He applied his time to developing some of his research projects and took his family to the local beach for a short vacation.

THE ANNUAL RITUAL
—YET AGAIN!

THE FIRST ORDER OF BUSINESS was the annual department meeting, held at the start of the academic year. John Esposito, typical of his behavior at previous such events, had his menu and script ready for the performance. The ritual was usually held on a Friday afternoon so participants could "party" afterward. Alistair found this annual custom so disturbing, he often smoked a cigarette in advance to calm himself down—something he did rarely but found necessary to cope with such occasions. The yearly pantomime was never enjoyable.

The shabby conference room, decorated with a few old award plaques and fading photos of past chairmen, was again prepared, and members shuffled in, some more enthused than others. As always, Alistair could tell peoples' attitudes by where they tended to sit: the cheerleaders always sat at the table up near the chairman, newly present graduate students toward the other end, and the unimpressed in chairs set against the walls. And as usual, Alistair and Alex sat near the main door in case they became so nauseated, they had to leave.

John opened the meeting by welcoming everyone back after the summer, particularly the new faculty. He summarized the unit's achievements from last year, especially newly promoted and tenured faculty, and moved to report the enrollment data, always posed optimistically and portrayed either as stable or on an upward trajectory.

He emphasized, "Everything looks good at this point: the department, faculty, and students are all on the right track, and the dean continues to support us budget-wise as much as he can."

Big deal! thought Alistair.

How original! mused Alex.

At this point, the Insiders chimed in, echoing John's praise of positive progress but emphasizing that the department required much greater financial and personnel support from the dean if fame and fortune were to be achieved.

Arnold stressed, "Thanks for your efforts, John, but we need far more if we are to make real progress into the national rankings. It is so frustrating to be right on the cusp of fame but not quite have adequate resources to put us over the top."

The Radicals further reinforced this view by emphasizing the need to recruit an increased proportion of female and African-American faculty to enhance meaningful diversity, a policy supported by Alistair.

Allen piped up, as usual, to accentuate greater support for significant increases in the department's diversity, resources, and equality. He blurted out, "Hell, when *is* the damned dean actually going to give us what we need? We have been subject to constant delays and desperately need to move ahead on these matters. He keeps asking us to achieve more with less. What *is* his problem?"

The Manipulators agreed but stressed that any new hires should be high quality and not detract from the department's attempts to improve its rankings.

In contrast, the Supporters were more concerned with the department's substantive and professional development needs, emphasizing its graduate training needs and desire for constant, consistent improvement over time. Their voice of reason was always a welcome relief from the harsh, irritating demands of the others.

Alex turned to Alistair and whispered, "Don't they know we have to be the best sociology department in town?"

They both found restraint difficult but managed to control their mirth until after the meeting, bristling at the self-delusion of their colleagues.

Alistair's exasperation was beginning to mount to new levels. His tone and facial expressions reflected increasing irritation: he often became extremely flushed, his eyes rolling, his lips twisted in anger. All this took a serious toll on his health. His impatience and cynicism became difficult to restrain, and he became concerned that he might experience an inappropriate public outburst. After all, he was beginning to blurt out his frustrations with the place and his infuriating colleagues to more than just Alex, a new habit that concerned him. His constant overreactions risked making him a target. He needed to be more careful and restrained. Reminding his fellow faculty they were "ridiculous idiots" would only work further against him, placing him in danger of becoming a major scapegoat. He clearly didn't want that but found restraining himself in public increasingly close to impossible.

When questions were invited, several graduate students spoke up, with the chair of their student union complaining, "We truly lack adequate financial support, are ignored when it comes to providing regular course offerings, and desperately need more help finding jobs. Is anything being done to help us?" Behind the scenes, Jack had often expressed the students' general frustration with John's general inaction regarding their concerns, despite endless promises. He met with Alistair from time to time, making him aware of levels of student frustration similar to the latter.

John responded, "Rest assured, we are all doing the very best we can to support you and frequently request more financial resources from the dean but with only limited success. However, we always have your best interests at heart, and my door is always open to talk. Please come by whenever you like." The ensuing silence reflected the audience's cynicism. Alistair and Alex silently groaned at this obvious, totally ineffective assertion. John's reactions matched the two friends' obvious language; they were totally vacuous and ineffective, intended primarily to appease the crowd.

Other faculty stressed that the students' concerns were all being addressed and told them to contact their graduate director for further information if necessary. This kind of mollifying nonresponse was designed to ensure their passivity and democratic image of the department generally.

Allen, as the leading Radical, was not satisfied by this response and complained that graduate students required collective bargaining and union representation to ensure their needs were met. John responded that the university was presently "looking into" this possibility and, for the moment, maintained tenuous peace.

A couple of other faculty asked how graduate enrollment might be increased, followed by discussion of training grant support and convincing the dean to provide more funding. As usual, no practical arrangements were made to obtain this support, and the discourse ended in empty generalities. Once the committees had presented their largely positive reports, the meeting adjourned to the lounge for the so-called "Happy Hour" of the week—an oxymoron indeed!

Retiring briefly to Alistair's office, the two friends discussed what had transpired at the meeting.

"Why do you imagine the annual department meeting has to be such an exercise in simplistic idealism?" asked Alex.

"In some ways, it is all very simple," answered Alistair. "Since sociologists' contact with reality is so indirect and their egos so fragile, they are forced to construct a positive group image of themselves to make them feel better, largely based on vacuous statements, regardless of the actual reality. What a waste of time all of this is—it could be dealt with in a memo!"

He continued, "As for the Happy Hour's awkwardness, I believe that in these unstructured situations, our colleagues, except when comfortably in their networks, really don't know how to act socially in a natural way. They tend to be hesitant and uncomfortable."

They both left to "socialize."

"Socializing"

THE FACULTY LOUNGE SPORTED a makeshift bar containing a flashing beer sign, and some upbeat music played from an old speaker. While some decorations appeared minimally appropriate, others seemed tacky, worn, and out of place given their age. No one could possibly mistake this artificial joviality for genuine hospitality.

Alistair and Alex had reluctantly decided to take a quick look and observe the departmental social scene, such as it *ever* was. They blurted out a few phrases of their secret language to some of the present faculty, who were obviously completely unaware of their linguistic game. Subjects such as the weather, new football team, state politics, and Ocala's possible budget—particularly faculty raises—dominated their empty everyday speech.

Typical phrases included remarks such as:

"Will this fall weather ever end? When will summer finally arrive?"

"How about the new coach and football team this year? Do you think they have a chance of a national championship?"

"While our state legislators talk a good game, will they ever actually give us the resources we need to move ahead?"

"After all these years of waiting, will desperately needed faculty raises actually happen?"

"When will Ocala become one of the top twenty best public universities?"

"All we need now are the resources!"

"Just give us the money, and we will get the job done!"

Nothing was lost except true communication, but nothing was gained either. Real conversation and interaction were totally lost in the banality of utterly empty phrases.

Predictably, the Insiders were at the center of things, laughing it up and carrying on as though they were actually attending a party. References to the faculty meeting were kept to a minimum, except among the Insiders who complained that not enough effort was being made to advance faculty and academic development. They made rumblings about looking for another chair ... one of themselves, perhaps? The Supporters tried to participate as best they could in a positive way, agreeing to John's leadership, at least for another year. A few of the Marginal showed up to put in a polite appearance but only stayed for a short visit. In general, such faculty situations were entirely awkward and artificial. These occasions conformed to Alistair's "Law of Opposites"; sociologists were largely socially inept and demonstrated this in their halting, awkward attempts at merriment.

Alistair and Alex made a minimal appearance and then retired to Alistair's cell—or office—to dissect the day's events.

The former began with, "As usual, we correctly predicted who leapt onstage the most, and what they might say."

His friend responded, "We also accurately anticipated that nothing significant would be discussed, debated, or decided during this annual ritual. This yearly ceremony possesses no real substance, representing the overture before the opera, the drum rolls before announcements, the menu presented before the meal. This imposed establishment model of departmental reality is refreshed every fall and offered to the faculty for their unthinking consumption and support."

Alistair readily agreed.

In contrast, John had beamed with satisfaction that he had pulled off yet another successful performance during the meeting. He was "*needed* by everyone" as *usual*. He felt proud and fulfilled.

He gloated and went around smiling broadly, greeting everyone individually during the "happy" hour as he sought further praise for bringing off yet another successful "show." His insecurity and need for social approval were obvious and endless.

"These occasions are so artificial, they can be neither enjoyed nor spontaneous; people don't know how to act and tend to express discomfort with each other," Alex continued. "Why?"

"I believe it's because the social situation is informal and unstructured," Alistair replied. "Whereas our colleagues are so used to managing their actions when *on*stage, they are at a loss *off*stage."

"No wonder these events are entirely empty and unenjoyable. No one knows how to act."

"Even alcohol helps little in these disasters, unfortunately."

Alistair returned home in disgust, eagerly looking forward to his evening Scotch.

Hiring Issues

As THE ACADEMIC YEAR PROCEEDED, a number of issues arose that frequently demanded attention. One of these involved hiring new personnel, which often became awkward and controversial. Alistair felt that recruiting represented a kind of "cloning" process; given their sensitive egos, faculty tended to project their professional self-images onto others, identifying those most similar to themselves while rejecting others who were clearly different.

He thought back to the previous year, when David had hired him to teach a graduate course the department badly needed. His visit and interview were both positive and hospitable, with little evidence of manipulation or politics behind the scenes. He settled in quickly and easily, playing a number of constructive roles, grateful for the opportunities offered to him. Back then, faculty were evaluated and rewarded for their general productivity without imposing unrealistic performance and publication expectations. However, over time, the atmosphere changed, becoming increasingly fine-tuned based on invidious distinctions regarding types of research and publication outlets. Once invented, citation indexes became increasingly relevant to a person's perceived professional reputation and productivity.

Sometime later, the new provost sought to sweep some weak faculty positions, two of which were located in sociology. This caused major resistance since these colleagues were close friends of others in their own department. The Insiders were among those close to the two faculty in question and started to lobby the departmental evaluation committee and chair to rescue their friends. Alistair, as an incoming chair, however, was not as enthusiastic and felt they could do better. They asked if he could forward their positive recommendation to the dean; the chair agreed but indicated he intended to forward his own, which differed from theirs. They were extremely displeased. They attempted to bypass the department and go straight to the dean.

When the provost caught wind of this, he was outraged and terminated both faculty immediately. So much for academic politics reflected in attempted end runs and influence peddling.

Pathetic and ineffective, thought Alistair as he watched his colleagues' attempts at manipulation fail spectacularly.

Affirmative action also offered opportunities to recruit and was highly attractive since it provided the department with additional faculty lines. Eventually, candidates were brought in to interview, largely from the South. They were welcomed, treated politely, and examined intensely at seminars presented to the department.

Allison, an African-American doctoral candidate, was a promising recent recruit. She related well to people in the department, including senior colleagues. Alistair tried to help her as best he could, supporting her promotion and encouraging her to pursue her career enthusiastically. She moved forward for promotion but was, unfortunately, unsuccessful in gaining tenure. So, after teaching at the African-American university across town for several years, she stopped working there to support her family.

After Allison's eventual termination, the two friends gathered in Alistair's office to discuss the general topic of recruitment.

Alex asked, "Why is this always such a twisted, competitive process?"

"Friends like to hire friends or allies in their networks. In any event, they definitely aren't interested in anyone who might 'threaten' or detract from their fragile egos," answered Alistair. "The cloning process is involved in the whole effort. Faculty aim to hire those who match and enhance their professional self-images and don't compete with them in any way."

"You're right!" Alex responded. "This also applies to affirmative action, in which our colleagues, rather than encouraging diversity, are seeking further clones of themselves."

"It's all about *self, self, self.* Self-enhancement, self-gain, self-interest, selfishness totally," Alistair added.

"Pathetic when you can see it for what it really represents."

Other major hiring issues arose during the 1990s when incoming chair Ian Evans's desire to hire his friends would cause significant resistance, anger, and pressure among local faculty. Instead of requesting they be considered and, if approved, allowed to transfer to Ocala, the usual national search process was imposed, including visits and interviews. Alistair was outraged, particularly since neither candidate appeared to fit the department's needs at that time. He checked with the dean of faculties to ensure proper hiring procedures were being followed, and supposedly, they were. It was at this point, he discovered the process was rigged; provided the formal system was followed—including general advertising, appropriate selection committees, and interviews—any predecided selection could be made regardless of other candidates in the hiring pool, in this case, as long as the Manipulators could control the outcome.

Consequently, James Griswold and his spouse were both hired and later tenured without difficulty. So much for transparency. While some approved of their roles in the department, others did not. The couple eventually moved elsewhere.

In this matter, the former dean, Christopher Jones, was also involved in the late 1980s, encouraging Ian as incoming chair, hoping he could bring the department together and improve it significantly. However, the possibility of significant progress was as likely as stopping a whirlpool. Additionally, the Insiders and Radicals supported the new chair, hoping he accomplished his goals. Alistair and Alex, on the other hand, found the process of importing new colleagues they neither liked nor trusted both twisted and nauseating.

Hiring and firing were obviously ideological and *not* objective matters—Alistair's disgust was mounting.

Graduate Student Questions

DEALING WITH GRADUATE STUDENT matters could also be frustrating. During 1983, Alistair was about to attend yet another meeting of the year's Graduate Program Committee—an arena for endless discussion, debate, and, on occasion, conflict. Why? Graduate students were often extensions of faculty egos and their personal sponsorship. Sometimes, apprentice-type relations developed in which major professors worked closely with their wards, absorbing them into their daily activities and identities. Those directing training programs also possessed vested interests in the academic and ongoing success of their graduate assistants, requiring them to perform well and move through their programs as quickly as possible. Graduate students, in turn, invested significant parts of themselves into their departments of choice, placing their own egos "on the line." This had particularly been the case during the decades of "democratization," during which graduate students temporarily became members of all departmental committees. Such encounters became rather like wrestling matches with participants jumping into the "ring" to sponsor, defend, and support their own candidates.

Some of the more traditional faculty, including the Supporters and, in some cases, the Manipulators, argued to "hold the line" on "standards" and retain conventional types of student evaluations. In response, many student representatives rejected this, lobbying instead to have acceptable course grades serve in the place of conventional evaluation methods.

Alistair, having been subject to extensive comprehensive exams himself, argued strongly for their retention, emphasizing the candidates' need for broad preparation prior to such events. He stressed, "Graduate courses, while an important part of training, can't substitute for thorough preparation. They are too limited in scope. Each candidate needs to prepare themselves as fully as possible before they take the exams."

A few of his colleagues supported this view; however, when too many students started to fail some of the program's core area exams, pressure was brought to pass more of them and implement the course grade system, which was eventually adopted.

The next day, outraged at this weakening of standards, Alistair went to visit the university's graduate committee chair. She listened calmly and then informed him that each department was free to adopt its own procedures, and the course grade system was acceptable. He left her office in disgust and informed Alex of this further reinforcement of academic mediocrity.

He emphasized, "While strong students will jump successfully through whatever hoops they face with little complaint, the more marginal spend excessive energy trying to dilute their program requirements instead."

Another sensitive area was graduate student admissions, particularly special student and minority group exceptions to normal criteria. Grade point averages were fairly minor issues— GRE scores, academic reputations, and letters of recommendation were more central. In this matter, the Radicals, Marginal, Supporters, and Critics all tended to be more tolerant than the Insiders or Manipulators, wanting opportunities to be more open and diverse and giving those from weaker academic backgrounds a chance at an academic career. This was often the case with successful undergraduates they knew well. Again, however, issues of "standards," "quality," "reputation," and "improvement" came into play, often causing emotional and divisive exchanges.

Another crackpot idea invented some decades back involved "take home" doctoral comprehensive exams, in which candidates were given one day per subject to complete core area exams applied to their major areas, permitting access to any materials they desired. This was implemented for several semesters until the results proved worse than traditional tests and the new arrangement abandoned. A number of students, quite strong in other ways, submitted exam papers that were little more than literature summaries and failed to address the questions asked.

Graduate program recruitment and policies figured next in the two friends' discussion. Alistair started with, "Again, faculty egos dominate this committee and its activities. Recruiting, sponsoring, mentoring, and graduating students at this level involve extensions of faculty selves. Consequently, they fight fiercely to have their way to protect and enhance themselves."

Alex concurred, emphasizing, "Look at the marginal and, in some cases, obnoxious students we have experienced who were protected and facilitated by their mentors going to incredible lengths to do so. A few spectacular cases included students who became obnoxious and threatening when asked to revise their theses or dissertations."

Looking back on all this, Alistair and Alex were cynically amazed as always, shaking their heads at the irrationality of it all. Unfortunately, manipulating standards and evaluation procedures became a matter of strategy when student success rates declined. Where was the academic integrity in all this? The degree to which vested interests diluted program requirements disturbed Alistair and Alex, but apparently not anyone else. They stared at the spectacle in wonder while their personal frustrations mounted.

Electing the Chair

ELECTING A NEW DEPARTMENT CHAIR every few years—or selecting the next "sacrificial lamb," as the two friends termed it—could also prove challenging. David's term as chair had come to an end earlier in 1971, not long after he hired Alistair. As a Supporter, he had proved to be a stable, effective, professional, and confident administrator who listened to his colleagues' opinions but also kept his own council. Next came John, whose insecure, approval-seeking, weak leadership constantly wavered, depending on which way the faculty wind blew. Consequently, he was largely ineffective.

Eventually, John was so looking forward to stepping down at the end of 1974, he arranged a string of paper clips, one for each day left in his term, which he kept in front of him in his office to symbolize the countdown. The position of chair was ironic in that most strong candidates steered away from it, not wanting to occupy it for long, often leaving the weak and desperate in line for the position, and assigning it more significance than it possessed.

James followed John as chair at the start of the 1974 academic year. He again typified the traditional authoritarian male desiring to be popular with both sides and obtain approval of the dean. He did not receive the chair selection committee's unanimous approval, but since stronger candidates rejected the possibility, he was sent forward for faculty approval. He tried to develop consensus and gain the approval of his colleagues, but his latent desire for control was always evident, working to his disadvantage. He was also not always consistent in his evaluation of and support for other faculty in matters of hiring, promotion, and tenure.

During the late 1970s, departmental support waned, and people looked forward to the end of his tenure. He was totally unaware of his downward slide in support and desperately desired renewal of his appointment for a second term. His colleagues moved to replace him, and Alistair was a member of the selection committee. Strangely, Esposito, despite his previous relief at stepping down, strongly desired to be reappointed to the position. A number of committee members were horrified by this prospect, and the search for alternative candidates commenced.

Alistair had also found James's simplistic authoritarian personality highly offensive and spoke out regarding what he felt the department's developmental needs were in some detail, emphasizing leadership was more important than imposed control. Further discussion led the committee to view Alistair as a possible chair candidate despite his membership on the selection committee. During this initial organizational meeting held during the latter part of James's administration, he had made some suggestions regarding the department's future direction that some members, apparently, felt helpful. Naïvely, he viewed the position as possibly attractive and, as is typical of the inexperienced, foolishly felt he could accomplish what others had failed to achieve.

At the end of James's term in 1978, Alistair became a candidate for the position and the committee forwarded his name for approval. John was personally outraged, viewing some of his colleagues as traitors, while James chastised Alistair for failing to appreciate everything he had tried to do for him in the past. Alistair assumed the position with marginal faculty approval.

Upon succession in 1979, he was immediately stereotyped as a tool of his own network and the dean, and was expected to act in a biased fashion, serving their own interests only rather than the department as a whole. This rapidly became the worst experience of his life as he suffered the suspicion, antagonism, pettiness, and opposition of most of his colleagues. All his efforts to improve the department academically were met with criticism and energetic attempts to block his desired improvements. Whatever he attempted to improve, he could do no right in the eyes of his colleagues. Because of their suspicions and distorted interpretations, all his efforts were largely in vain. It was a lose-lose situation. He was disgusted, and so was Alex.

Alistair became so stressed, he developed even more health problems, and his hair turned completely gray. Additionally, he hated to retire for the night because he knew he had to return to the office the next morning. He experienced aspects of faculty behavior he wished he had never known; *nothing* was beyond personal pettiness. While his friends supported him, the rest opposed whatever he attempted, casting dark aspersions on his assumed motives. In the midst of all this, he attempted to maintain stability and treat everyone fairly.

Gradually, this "descent into hell" became too much for him; he had decided to resign from the position, despite some encouragement to remain, at the end of 1977, his first and last year as chair. Sometimes, trying to "do the right thing" had proven too much. Immediately after he announced his resignation, those waiting to take over appeared on the scene. The Insiders started to agitate, and Andrew, one of the Insiders, soon advertised his desire to take over.

Alistair and Alex both groaned.

The former complained, "Insider Andrew will be little more than a number-crunching, bureaucratic member of the Insiders, supporting his friends, adding to the already high level of their unrealistic cheerleading."

Alex agreed and sympathized; there appeared to be little they could do to avoid this return to "normal."

Thus commenced the regime of the self-appointed Insiders, acting as the "Pied Pipers of Hambrook," leading their "children" into Ocala Valley through the Heavenly Gates to the Eden of the Famous Department. Arnold followed Andrew as chair in the late

1970s and early 1980s, repeating his positive babble about the unit's needs constantly to the dean, measuring each perceived rating increase microscopically. During all this, the Supporters gave their encouragement when justified, the Radicals continued to lobby for their own rewards and policy changes, the Manipulators largely remained aloof, and the Marginal remained potentially vulnerable.

Later, with Ian as an outside chair in 1982, the atmosphere increasingly had become more invidious, aggravated when he imported some of his friends. The Critics never gave their approval to these intrusions and began to act as the underground opposition. Fortunately, the chair position eventually became somewhat more neutral, rotating around the senior faculty with little disagreement or conflict. As the intervening scapegoat, the chair's position was recognized as less than enviable.

Looking back on all this, Alistair well recalled his colleagues' manipulations and attempts at dominance. Anger and resentment, based on unsatisfied expectations, never disappeared; it just waited in the wings. Alistair had been seriously "burned" by his one-year chair experience, requiring a long period and extensive therapy to recover, then only minimally. The two friends reminisced about how bad John Esposito had been, how unfortunate James was as his unwelcome replacement, Alistair's regrettably abortive attempt at the role, and the Insiders' dismally ineffective performances thereafter. Eventually, chair occupants largely "took their turn" as senior faculty members, with significantly lowered expectations. Both Alex and Alistair commented on how those who had never experienced the position previously automatically assumed they could run the place better than current occupants since they listened to their egos rather than their minds. At this point, the position became largely part of the administrative system and lost much of its dynamic potential.

Annual Evaluations

ANNUAL EVALUATIONS—or "Yearly Virility Tests," as Alistair called them—began in the spring toward the end of each academic year. Alistair experienced his first of these at the end of his 1971 academic year. They were used to make salary recommendations when raises were available. They also served as indices of progress toward promotion and tenure. When Alistair had first arrived on campus, these deliberations were calm, considerate, and reasonable; committee members looked to recognize and reward faculty where possible. During Alistair's earlier years at Ocala during the 1970s, a fairly consistent hierarchy of faculty rating "high," "medium," and "low" for raises had emerged but was not viewed as fixed. Attempts were made to praise individuals for whatever achievements they had attained, encouraging them to achieve more in the future. However, once the Mafia achieved power, the game changed greatly, particularly when the department was encouraged by external forces and conditions to become more successful grants-wise and in academic reputation.

Alistair never forgot the day Mafia Ian leered into his face, delighting in "how the mighty have fallen," based on the Critic's failure to be recommended for a raise.

Ian screeched, "Your special relationship with the dean is now a thing of the past!"

Alistair barely managed to contain himself in the face of such a vicious attack, filing this incident in the back of his memory to avenge later. He had *never* been treated in such an insulting manner.

Such appraisals became much more than examining a person's record; they also reflected that individual's position in the network. Department and committee meetings became cheerleader sessions in which Ian encouraged and, on occasion, *demanded* that everyone "pull their weight" to make this the "best sociology department in the South." The evaluation process became increasingly microscopic, using a variety of comparative data to examine a faculty member's teaching, publication record, and, to a much lesser extent, service work to the department and university—the least valued of all three.

Once during the mid-1970s, Alex had been called out by then-chair James as unproductive when Alex had actually written and presented a number of research papers at several conferences, some of them international. Alex immediately went down to the dean to harangue him for this injustice, and in loud terms. Alex screamed at the dean, "You clearly don't know what you are doing and should pay more attention to detail rather than relying on the comments of your ignorant chairs!" This was a lesson to be remembered. The dean apologized, and the negative designation was reversed.

Many decades later, a similar attack was made on Radical Nancy's creativity after a long illness and many years of nonproductivity. In that incidence, Alistair was a committee member and, while finding the effort disturbing, had agreed with the designation since she was granted so many years to turn her situation around.

Other major incidents included the encouragement to fire Hippie Mike, the rebel who had become an outsider, primarily for his attitude and, to a lesser extent, his behavior. Mafia Ian also critiqued Insider Max's work in great detail when he was considered for promotion and tenure, even having his staff assistant remove Max's doctoral dissertation from his office without his knowledge for detailed examination. Ian's assistant felt so uncomfortable about her forced actions, she quickly transferred out of the department. Despite such interference, the promotion and tenure committee evaluated Max's candidacy positively and promoted him.

Henry, a very weak, long-term department member, was highly unproductive, ineffective at teaching, and inefficient in completing administrative tasks. His annual duty assignments included increased teaching, despite his obvious limitations, and a short stint as assistant chair, at which he failed completely. Interestingly, since he had been in the department so long and had not been fired, he was permitted to limp along to retirement, even achieving "emeritus" status at that time. Henry had always "known his place," remaining quiet and compliant at all times. Such passivity at the "bottom of the pile" served him well later when his tenure was in jeopardy. His surprising fate illustrated the inconsistency and hypocrisy of the evaluation process.

Looking back on it all, Alistair was struck by the subjective nature of these appraisals. Quantity was one thing—and even in this regard, some faculty were lacking—while quality was at least somewhat in the eye of the beholder, reinforced by network contexts. Some candidates, at least two, were tenured based on the promise of forthcoming publications that never appeared. Alistair's absence of annual raises and tangible recognition fueled his outrage further. His resentment was rising to new heights.

Referring to annual evaluations generally, Alex, having been burned by the dean in the recent past, stressed how the process could become weaponized, politicized, and subject to administrative abuse. Each year, faculty were examined for their performance levels in their assigned duties and, if relevant, progress toward promotion and tenure. Since the evaluation committee was elected each year and the recommendations forwarded to the dean, outside influences could play a major part in the annual rankings and recommendations produced.

Promotion and Tenure:
Coronation or Crucifixion?

PROMOTION AND TENURE CONSIDERATIONS represented, perhaps, the most potentially conflict-ridden situations of all. They originated in the department's evaluation committee and moved to the general faculty, followed by university committee decisions and the provost's recommendations to the president. As with annual evaluations, network support was crucial.

Alistair attempted to evaluate candidates for their contributions to the department, discipline, and professions rather than their social popularity. Such an approach turned out to be far from the norm; many of his colleagues focused rather on their individual relations with candidates, how they were hired, and the extent to which they served their personal academic interests. During earlier decades, the department had only encouraged candidates they felt they could support to submit their portfolios for consideration. For the most part, few controversies arose and peace was maintained. As more faculty were involved, however, weaker individuals came up for consideration, causing increased controversy.

Alistair's past negative promotion experiences, particularly those reflecting the facilitation of friends and rejection of enemies, soon taught him how the game was played: candidates were either "in" or "out," and in the case of the evaluators' friends, they were supported unquestionably while outsiders were picked apart and rejected. Evaluations were almost always at one extreme or the other. While a few views were more moderate and tempered, others were extremely destructive, with crucifying personal attacks pouring "blood on the floor." In the latter cases, nominees had often offended the evaluators in some manner. In some cases, candidates were initially promoted but subsequently denied tenure. This reminded Alistair of the dehumanizing aspects of prejudice and discrimination, reflected in high levels of antagonism toward outgroup members, justified by negative stereotypes. For the most part, he kept silent during these rituals, evaluating and voting his conscience without regard to prevailing opinion. Instead of thorough and objective, the process reflected prevailing network ties or their absence.

During the late 1970s, the day had arrived to consider Vulnerable Roy, the family sociologist, for promotion and tenure, a decision that was to become a major event in the department's future welfare since it highlighted internal inconsistencies and hypocrisy in a most humiliating fashion. Alistair and Alex felt they might be attending an execution and dragged themselves into the depressing conference room, as usual, sitting against the wall as from the center of the "action" far as possible. All relevant faculty had been provided access to the candidate's folder in advance, containing his vita, duty assignments, teaching evaluations, publications, and letters of recommendation. Some completed their preparation for the process more meticulously than others, depending on their motives.

During the meeting, John had been in his element as chair, reading the formally prescribed rules that define the process, its legalities, and underlying collective bargaining agreements. He briefly summarized the details of the folder and opened the floor to discussion. Comments were seriously considered and recorded. Those supporting Roy's candidacy spoke in his favor, emphasizing his strong teaching and positive relations with students, both undergraduate and graduate. He had supervised a number of graduate theses and dissertations successfully and was well-liked. He had also contributed to committee work at department, college, and university levels. Colleagues such as James and Max felt Roy represented a fairly strong applicant and would continue to serve the department's needs in the future. His publication record, while limited, did contain a refereed article in a well-known journal, along with other reports, conference presentations, and unpublished papers.

At this point, however, the ritual had taken a negative turn; even some of Roy's supporters indicated their concerns regarding his limited productivity after so many years and wondered if this apparent weakness might continue after tenure. Others—particularly the Obnoxious—like sharks attracted by the smell of blood, went on the attack. Roy's refereed paper had been coauthored, and after almost seven years, he developed little more, barely moving beyond his dissertation research. The Supporters on the committee offered only mildly positive comments, also concerned with his research productivity. Additionally, he had obtained no grants, research- or training-oriented, and accordingly had contributed no financial support to the department's budgetary needs. The tone had definitely become more destructive and threatening, moving toward a negative outcome. Alistair and Alex, while not vocal, were not impressed either. Apparently, the detractors might win the day.

The atmosphere had become electric, and temporarily, silence reigned. Some were uncomfortable with these developments; others remained impatient to end the matter.

Allen had stated, "We appear to have reached a decision and need to move forward. While Roy has made some contributions to the department, his record unfortunately doesn't appear to justify his promotion."

Responding to this, John had tried to move the meeting forward by summarizing both positive and negative comments, accentuating the former more than the latter, concluding, "Roy has been a good colleague to us all, supported our graduate students and department needs, and been a good team member."

As Roy's supposed supporter, James had also tried to put the best face he could on the situation but clearly lacked enthusiasm. He stated, "While Roy has contributed to the department's welfare, I wish he had begun and pursued his research program earlier in his career. Unfortunately, his publication list, while including a few strong articles, is rather weak."

As it turned out, Roy had quickly learned that his supposed allies were two-faced and hypocritical regarding their support; while encouraging him to his face, they were more critical in their discussions with his colleagues and likely to vote against his tenure.

As a result of this rejection, he had felt alienated and deeply offended. How could his colleagues treat him in this hypocritical manner? Hadn't he tried his hardest to please them? What more could he have possibly done?

The chair, not wanting to offend anyone, had also encouraged committee members to be positive and constructive. Secret ballots were eventually distributed, requiring committee members to state reasons for any negative votes or abstentions. Alistair found this to be ridiculous and refused to comply, feeling this compromised the confidentiality of the process. John took the ballots to his office where, with Andrea's help, they were tallied and recorded. He returned to the conference room to announce the results. To his disappointment, the majority turned out to be negative but not overwhelmingly so.

Committee members had shuffled out slowly, returning to their respective kennels to ponder what had taken place. John later met with Roy to discuss this outcome and encouraged him to put himself up for promotion, regardless of the department's decision at this point. Roy decided to do so and was successful at the college level; however, his candidacy was later rejected by the university committee, much to his disappointment. He instead received a termination letter containing one-year's notice.

Roy had felt personally betrayed in light of all his intense efforts to complete his doctorate; move to Ocala; support the department, its faculty, and students; and establish his career. He found the rejection to be devastating and outrageous. How could he be treated so badly? Why did he deserve this? He began to plan his vengeance; he started working through his possible options for payback, ranging from the mild to the more radical, including destructive violence.

Alistair contemplated the inconsistent, disingenuous dynamics of the system: Supporters were often lukewarm or silent; others, given their own weak records, were hypocritical in their condemnations; while still others felt they were superior. While Alistair did not entirely disagree with the outcome in this case, he found it deeply troubling. Little did the faculty know the destructive consequences this decision was destined to have on the unit's future and their own careers. Ironically, the "game" was rigged from the start, largely based on the candidate's position within the department's social networks, as well as their general image. The potential for inaccurate, unfortunate outcomes, like jury decisions, was always high as a result.

Allison was a second case whose future at Ocala was in potential jeopardy. She had been welcomed by the faculty and became popular with the undergraduates who appreciated her distinctive views and experience on social issues. Her career moved forward well for some time: her teaching was welcomed, she provided service work for the department, college, and university, and initiated her writing program. After several energetic years, she assembled her file for promotion consideration, providing evidence of her publications, solid teaching, and service to the department and university. Alistair tried to help her with some of the publishing outlets familiar to him, finding her school racial ecological research both interesting and relevant to current issues. She was supported for promotion, and her candidacy moved to the next level. She was elated and felt her career was now on track. However, over time, she started to have health issues.

She had rallied later in the year and brought together her materials to be considered for tenure. This time, unfortunately, matters did not proceed so smoothly. While her teaching and service remained satisfactory, her record was thoroughly examined and critiqued by the Manipulators and Mafia, who concluded she did not meet minimum standards for tenure and voted her down. Others argued in support of diversity and what she brought to Ocala and its students, but they were in the minority. Since she was in his field, Alistair supported her strongly in the discussion, emphasizing the department's weak record on minority faculty recruitment. Nothing worked. Even her female colleagues voted Allison down since, in their view, she did not fit the mold of a professional academic. She moved to teach at the African-American university across town for a number of years before retiring early.

Alistair sat in the department conference room at the time, staring in amazement at all the destruction. Here again was yet another familiar crucifixion—extreme labeling and condemnation! Some of the Mafia's persistent comments regarding Allison's teaching and problematic publishing habits had dominated the discussion of her case. *Yet another travesty*, Alistair thought to himself as he submitted his positive vote, knowing full well he was in the minority. The two friends concluded it all came down to "academic politics as usual" and returned to their kennels in disgust, fully appreciating they could have been subject to similar unconscionable treatment by the Mob if they had ever been accorded the opportunity.

Alistair could not bring himself to leave, however, before the two of them had discussed recent promotion and tenure decisions, the most politicized of all aspects of the department. The two friends began with Roy's earlier case.

He emphasized, "I believe we both agree that Roy's candidacy was somewhat marginal and could have gone either way. What struck me most, however, was the hypocrisy of his supporters, some of whom spoke out of both sides of their mouths at the same time."

This brought them to Allison, another most unfortunate situation. While she had cooperated with some of the Mafia, accepting their help with methodological issues, she was never completely successful with refereed publication submissions.

Alistair wondered why she had not requested help from her major professor, particularly in light of his writing and publication rate of success. Her personal situation had also been aggravated by her mounting illness, and the end result was very disappointing.

Alistair emphasized, "Allison made a sincere effort to be successful despite the odds against her."

"Yet another lamb to the slaughter," concluded Alex.

Alistair, regretfully, had to agree. "Unless you are totally subservient to the Mafia," he added, "you get nowhere, regardless of affirmative action. It's more like *negative* action!"

Alex chuckled in cynical amusement.

They settled in to talk further.

Alex observed, "Obviously, regular tasks such as recruitment and graduate program matters are defined from an egocentric perspective, motivated by attempted cloning in some cases and stroking one's ego in others. Graduate students are part of this when admitted and sponsored as extensions of each major professor's self-identity. Also, when marginal, attempts may be made to ensure their progress through the program to graduation despite obvious weaknesses." He smiled, adding, "I ought to know."

"How about the dynamics of promotion and tenure? Now that's a topic you can really sink your teeth into!"

Alistair responded, "It's really no mystery. Those different from the in-group are often punished by being treated hypocritically, with condescension, ridicule, and outright rejection, particularly when they don't 'measure up,' don't fit in with the in-crowd, occupy competitive positions, are socially unpopular, or are appointed by outsiders. 'If you have done nothing for me lately, forget it! You have to reflect positively on *me* and be part of *my* network, or all is lost for you.'"

"It's truly pathetic how academics define the social world almost totally in relation to their insecure selves," Alistair said. "They project onto others and evaluate the images returned to them. So much for science and 'objectivity'!"

Alex concluded, "I agree that it's pitiful, but it won't change. I'm also amazed that so few negative consequences have occurred because of this."

He had no idea how wrong he was.

Further Musings

AFTER THE LAST PROMOTION AND tenure meeting, Alistair was enjoying his whiskey and soda at Alex's comfortable apartment. The latter sipped his bourbon. They began to reminisce about recent events in the department, not that they were unusual.

As they made themselves comfortable and chatted, Alistair harkened back to the department's annual meeting. "Can you believe how simplistic and idealistic this ritual has become?" he asked.

"Sure I can. Sociologists have fragile, insecure egos and only indirect contact with the outside world. They are compelled to project positive images of themselves, particularly as a group. Hence, they put the best face on things, looking to an optimistic future," Alex responded.

"I guess they combine this with constant demands for more resources and recognition from the dean since they feel constantly unrecognized and underappreciated."

Alex agreed. "Yes, and they also tend to talk in broad reputational generalities based on local comparisons rather than specifics since attention to detail doesn't make them look good. Focusing on the department's reputation as whole glosses over its weaker members. Repeatedly stating we are on an upward trajectory accomplishes little apart from annoyance."

Alistair laughed. A friend had once pointed out to him that annual sociology conferences served as places for academics to demonstrate their identities as social scientists. The actual content of the meetings meant little; the ritual itself was more important. In a similar vein, the annual faculty meeting dramatized what the department was all about as a group reality: flexing its muscles and voicing its imagined strengths, future developments, and endless needs.

Other faculty activities, including socializing, hiring, dealing with graduate students, chair elections, and faculty evaluations, were all tainted by network dynamics and which groups were dominant, particularly the Mafia along with the Manipulators and Insiders. Consequently, little evidence of actual academic freedom and tolerance existed. Furthermore, the decisions made at the end of such deliberations were often inaccurate and one-sided, seriously detracting from Ocala's long-term effectiveness. Many faculty were seriously lacking in self-awareness; consequently, they unconsciously permitted their prejudices and selfish motives to drive their perceptions of reality and consequent decisions. As a result, they were often extremely wrong and unfair but assumed the opposite!

The two friends continued to analyze the toxic atmosphere, marveling at the degree to which academics lacked self-awareness or political skills to actually bring about effective social change.

Alistair commented, "It's the blind leading the blind, thinking they can actually see!"

Alex responded, "If they *only* knew the full reality, although I seriously doubt this would slow them down."

The late afternoon was moving toward evening, and Alistair soon had to head home. They finished their drinks, and he departed, shaking his head in frustration.

PART THREE: THE CONSEQUENCES

THE 1989 ACADEMIC YEAR EVENTUALLY drew to a close, once again providing welcome relief for those who had suffered the usual vagaries of recent semesters. Few committee meetings of any kind occurred during the summer break, leaving faculty free to pursue their research, writing, and vacations at will and largely in isolation—the best aspect of all! Some with bruised egos had time to recover, at least partially. As time passed, both Alistair and Alex strongly resisted the prospect of fall just over the horizon. The beginning of yet another annual cycle was definitely *not* what they needed. But as the temperature and humidity rose inexorably in July, the new academic year loomed, and August approached. The usual rituals were about to repeat themselves. They both groaned and prepared to crawl back to campus.

The Mafia in Charge

THE YEAR 1990 PROMISED TO BE significantly more painful for the department with Mafia Ian at the helm. The two Critics anticipated much greater pressure on annual evaluations, promotion and tenure rituals, recruitment needs, and, in particular, the Insider cheerleading machine. The Insiders portrayed the department as more outstanding than it truly was, designed to ramp up demands for greater resources from the dean. They always painted themselves as superior to all others, filled with endless self-praise and demands for more resources. This refrain eventually rang hollow, impressing no one.

The Critics' performance, of course, went unrecognized. Alistair expected absolutely no professional recognition nor raises from the new in-group, while Alex wondered when and how he might be attacked by committee members.

The annual ritual was about to start, and the two friends moved toward the depressing conference room as slowly as possible, once again sitting as far away from the central table as they could. Most faculty eventually stumbled into the "theater," and the pantomime commenced. Boredom and a desire to flee as soon as possible reigned almost immediately. As anticipated, the chair's motivational speech was center stage, presented as vociferously as possible, designed to inspire the audience and boost their academic plans and performance. *He*, above all, was qualified to be their *true* leader; past chairs, by comparison, had been weak and relatively ineffective.

Ian concluded by stating, "I expect everyone to join me in taking a pledge to make this the best sociology department in the state, the South, and in the nation. This was my main goal in coming to Ocala, and I have promised the dean I will carry this out as soon as possible. Accordingly, you all need to boost your productivity, obtain external funding, master your teaching, and contribute significantly to the unit's expected meteoric rise to national fame. I expect all of you to 'put your shoulder to the wheel,' give it all your 'best shot,' and maximize your personal energy and application to the 'task at hand.'"

The two friends groaned at this turgid use of obvious language.

Alistair thought, *His boring, obvious comments are almost as impressive as ours. However, he is completely unaware of it and takes it seriously! What a farce!* He whispered to Alex, "I wonder when Hollywood will start calling!"

Those present were required to "take the oath of commitment to departmental development" and nodded affirmatively, as though they were members of a cult. The similarity, in fact, was uncanny; perhaps Jonestown was on the horizon. The atmosphere was growing tense.

Alistair turned to Alex again and whispered, "Could he be more mundane? Doesn't he know we are already the best sociology department in town?"

Alex could barely hold himself together, exclaiming, "Hollywood couldn't improve on this! Ian is so good at spewing vacuous, simplistic, meaningless phrases, he is starting to contribute to our dull language. We should award him a prize—the Golden Idiot Award!"

Alistair responded, "Yes! It's hilarious."

During the remainder of the meeting, the raised enthusiasm level was further reflected in the reports of major committee chairs. *Everything* was wonderful and would be even more so if only the administration recognized the faculty for what they were and doubled their resources. Everyone's blindness and fantasies continued unabated.

Where have I heard this refrain before? thought Alistair cynically. *If the resources were doubled, they would simply be squandered.*

At the end of all the presentations, a few questions were raised concerning how best to implement Ian's mandates; as always, these evoked vacuous generalities, and everyone prepared to retire to the "Happy Hour"—an obvious misnomer.

Most of the faculty moved across the hall to begin the "festivities." On this occasion, there was more than an ample supply of alcohol, including wine and beer, and music to encourage participants to enjoy themselves and socialize. The Insiders were beginning to "whoop it up" while the Mafia did their best to follow in their wake. A few of the Marginal also attended, looking distinctly uncomfortable and leaving soon after arrival. The noise level started to pick up while beer and wine consumption increased significantly—a clear contrast to previous such events.

The two friends participated on the sidelines as best they could and then retired to one of their cells to share observances.

"Quite the spectacle," Alex commented, and Alistair agreed.

"With both the Insiders and Mafia ramping things up and fueled by alcohol, it's reached a level I've never seen before," Alistair concluded. "Not that it's genuine."

"Forced joviality imposed largely by Insiders celebrating their assumed power achievements," agreed Alex.

The room became so loud, eventually the partiers could no longer hear each other.

The "Erotic" Scene

ALEX AND ALISTAIR DECIDED the day had been long and painful enough; after discovering Alex had forgotten to collect some paperwork from the secretary, they returned via the front office to the elevator. At first, everything seemed quiet. After a moment, however, soft giggling could be heard coming from Ian's office. Alex cracked the large door open slowly. To his amazement, he saw Ian and Andrea, the chair's assistant, engaged in *delicto flagrante* on the worn carpet. They were groaning and rutting like minks. Strands of gray hair littered the couch and floor, along with their clothing. While the room was largely cloaked in darkness, evidence of recent events was clearly visible. The scene was utterly dumbfounding, leaving the audience speechless.

Alex gestured to Alistair to come over and look. The latter gasped in surprise, equally amazed and greatly amused by the astonishing scene. *We couldn't wish for anything better than this!* he thought. He speculated that too much alcohol had been enjoyed by both participants, aggravated by Andrea's apparently sexless marriage over countless years. The obvious disturbance had attracted more faculty who now watched in amazement. The sight was hardly erotic; indeed, most spectators were repulsed and quickly withdrew after shielding their eyes as much as possible. Both friends felt this was the most suitable ending to an annual department travesty they had ever experienced, joking endlessly as they all headed home. For *once*, they were able to contemplate the day's events with some enjoyment.

News of the tryst quickly reached the dean. Despite having his own weaknesses and proclivities, he suspended both Ian and Andrea for three months to facilitate a dean of faculty investigation of their behavior. While no prude, he was not going to condone such "moral turpitude." Someone from another department was appointed temporary chair in the meantime.

The administration carried out an extensive investigation of the incident and, eventually, terminated both parties. Ian's wife divorced him, and he was forced into early retirement; Andrea moved on to distant locations out west without her husband. She didn't regret her behavior.

Alistair and Alex could not have been more pleased—satisfaction at last, and they had played absolutely no part in *any* of it! The department's downward rush to infamy had begun. Finally, things were beginning to pick up in Alistair's eyes; however, this was only temporary.

Roy's Termination

THE DEPARTMENT'S PATH TO self-destruction was accelerated by Roy Jackson's termination, which had left him extremely bitter. His final year was about to end. He felt he had done his best to fit in and contribute to the department: He had achieved success in teaching at all levels and had begun to publish in refereed outlets. He had worked hard for years to contribute to the department and place himself strongly within it. And he had performed well socially and academically. What *more* did they want? Many of his colleagues had encouraged him, claiming they supported his promotion, but it was all a lie. Their revealed hypocrisy and "forked tongues," only added to his rage.

At first, he tried to step back from the situation to assess matters as clearly and objectively as possible. Given the years of serious effort he had made, he felt helpless and hopeless in this situation. No wonder he felt he was losing his mind! Everything around him was out of control, and at this point, few, if any, positive options occurred to him.

Looking at his own life, he felt a sense of hopelessness. Ironically, despite specializing in family sociology, he had experienced two divorces and still was not doing well in his personal life. His finances were also in disarray. *Is there anything left worth a damn?* he wondered. *Why has this happened to me? I'm hardly worse than anyone else!*

As his last day drew near, Roy searched the job market only to find that in his case, it was not promising at all; the few opportunities available were offered in other specialties and at very limited institutions. Indeed, the future appeared entirely grim. So why not go out in a blaze of glory?

He gave the prospect some thought and decided to take a weekend trip out of town to ponder his plans. He drove to the closest beach and spent a couple of days sunbathing, reading for pleasure, and enjoying the surf. While he managed to relax, the back of his mind was preoccupied with devious ideas. The weekend went by rapidly, and in no time, he was reluctantly on his way home. There he found some legal mail awaiting him, containing provocative divorce settlement proposals from his last wife, financial matters, and a variety of bills. It was as though he had never left; his rage and depression immediately returned with a fury.

He thought through a wide variety of options, ranging from the highly violent, such as killing his colleagues through torching the building, to milder actions, including different forms of protest to maximize sociology's negative image. After calm consideration, he decided to fund an in-depth investigation of the department's core faculty.

After elaborate research, he searched out a private investigator highly experienced with academic cases and met with him to plan "the project" in detail. They focused on the department's central faculty, delineating a number of major issues and possible data sources the investigator might explore. Roy particularly focused on the hypocritical manner in which he had been treated and the department's corrupt practices. The consultant promised to get back to him soon with an initial draft. They met again soon to outline the project's goals, methods, and possible data sources. While such a project consumed extra time and money, Roy felt this was the most appropriate way to seek retaliation.

During the days that followed, Roy continued to function as best he could, greeting his colleagues politely, teaching his classes seriously, serving on committees, and simultaneously exploring job possibilities beyond the purely academic, such as social work or counseling, neither of which appealed to him. At the week's end, however, he felt as though he had fallen off a cliff; the black cloud of misery returned, and his plans to take revenge moved toward implementation.

After working through a list of appropriate venues to inflict his destruction on those who had injured him so badly, Roy decided his target group would be the department's next meeting, scheduled a few months out, where they all planned to discuss their Stalinist-like five-year plan.

Having planned this out in detail, Roy sat back and pondered his intentions. What might this achieve for him? It could possibly end his career. Was such extreme "payback" what the situation really called for? How might he be remembered? Might any of his enemies learn anything from this extreme act? He backed off his strategy, at least temporarily, considering other types of action, including those less controversial or potentially damaging.

At night in particular, he thought through his intentions in detail, playing out each part of them along with their possible consequences. In the end, he asked the major question: Why did this proposed action appeal to him so greatly? Other than simple revenge, he had no clear answer. On the other hand, he felt he *had* to respond to those who had wronged him so badly.

The Investigation

EVENTUALLY, ROY FELT HE HAD prepared enough and was ready to take the next step. The intervening months passed by rapidly, during which he vacillated somewhat between showing up and remaining home. Once the final investigative report was drafted, edited, and finalized, however, he decided to proceed.

After a full breakfast, he approached Hambrook slowly and entered his office, closing the door behind him. He waited silently for 10 a.m. to come around, still pondering his options. As he thought of what he had suffered, however, he became increasingly enraged and was fully prepared to act. He walked slowly down to the conference room his face grim.

As he entered, several colleagues, feeling guilty no doubt, greeted him warmly with false enthusiasm. He responded minimally and without smiling, taking a seat at the table, positioning himself as close to his targets as possible. Others slithered in slowly until the majority were present, including Alistair and Alex, whose encouragement he had always appreciated. He felt he was in a black hole. The interim chair initiated the meeting by announcing the major planning topics to be considered. As was customary, these included budgets, enrollment, recruitment possibilities, and faculty achievements. Roy waited patiently, hearing none of the boring discussion. The usual participants made their expected comments; he knew little might actually be achieved.

After about thirty minutes, he could wait no longer and raised his hand. He was recognized almost immediately. "As you will all recall," he said calmly, "this is my final year at Ocala due to your rejection of my candidacy for promotion and tenure. Initially, I was treated fairly and positively. Recently, however, I feel I have been subjected to unduly harsh, negative, and inconsiderate criticism. My achievements in all aspects were rejected, and so was I. Since my appeals were all unsuccessful, I felt I had no alternative but to take action.

"Consider this: while my limited salary is about to end, I decided to spend a significant part of my remaining funds on an investigation of the department's major faculty. I hired a national academic investigator who carried out his research in great detail, based on extensive information, and produced an interesting but damning report. You'll be happy to know that results are about to appear in our local newspaper, and copies have been forwarded to the dean as well as several ethics boards administered by regional and national professional sociological associations. The report, based on significant and fully documented evidence, contains striking evidence of illegal, corrupt, and unethical activities performed by several individuals in our department. Some of its major conclusions indicate that:

"Allen's latest boat and automobile purchases were funded by monies from his research grants.

"John has been involved in multiple affairs with his teaching and graduate assistants.

"Jim Foulds is currently under scrutiny for sexual harassment on a number of his staff. Human resources is particularly interested in these accusations.

"Arnold, our esteemed interim chair, has successfully—until now—hidden his previous convictions for DUIs incurred prior to moving to Ocala. He is currently pursuing a divorce *and* is being audited for alleged misuse of department funds.

"Jim Griswold has received several highly critical reviews of his papers that suggest major parts of them are unoriginal an unsourced.

"Some of Andrew's major computer banks contain false, artificial data. And on a more personal level, his credit report appears highly problematic, approaching bankruptcy.

"Arnold is fighting off a few student accusations that some of his major works were actually coauthored with them but not published as such.

"Nancy's current spouse has been engaging in multiple affairs successfully hidden from her and other family members.

"And finally, a couple of degree qualifications of some of the senior faculty are being examined for authenticity, particularly Allen.

"Past hiring, funding, and tenure cases are also being reexamined for evidence of possible corruption. There are a few minor offenses committed by other colleagues, but the ones just mentioned constitute the report's primary conclusions."

At this point, he fobbed off any reactions from his audience.

"Ironically, while I am deemed unworthy of tenure at Ocala, many of my colleagues are far more unqualified in legal terms, sufficient to justify dismissal. Many of you now face the possible termination of your careers and likely destruction of the department. This constitutes the ultimate hypocrisy, though, ironically, it should grant you the widespread publicity you all so desperately desire and, frankly, deserve."

At this point, Roy sat down calmly and waited quietly.

The atmosphere was electric but deafeningly silent. Most sat completely shocked, staring at the floor. Eventually, a few protested their rage and innocence of the published charges, threatening to sue Roy for everything he possessed and more.

Allen was particularly outraged. "Who the hell do you think you are, questioning my grant records and degree? You don't even have tenure!"

Others, including John, could not believe their ears and barked out their denials and rage, also threatening to sue for damages. Tears started to well up in the eyes of some while others buried their faces in their hands.

Roy laughed, screaming, "Sue all you like! You have ensured my long-term poverty, and there is nothing to gain!"

Others named in the report protested their denials, contesting both the accusations and documented evidence. They loudly proclaimed their innocence and denounced his actions, using terms such as "nonsense," "fantasy," "malice," "insanity," "distortion," and "projection."

The Vulnerable remained silent, as did the Critics and Supporters; however, the Insiders and Mafia loudly objected and proclaimed their innocence. They questioned the validity of the investigative data as well as Roy's motives in commissioning the report. In their eyes, he was simply looking for revenge instead of accepting his fate as expected. Labels such as "immature," "selfish," "punitive," and "jealous" were tossed around the room until all attendees had exhausted their rage.

Eventually, people began to leave the conference room in silence, mumbling in threatening tones. Some approached him, arguing that the evidence was inaccurate, or that the report should not be published; he should simply accept the fact he had not made it at Ocala State. They attempted to engage him in debate, challenging his accusations and evidence. Allen was particularly outraged, denying all accusations and supposed evidence. However, Roy refused to respond, gathered his materials, and exited the room silently.

He traveled quickly to his largely empty apartment to pack his few remaining possessions. After completing this, he climbed into his SUV and began his trip back home to Alaska to stay with his parents as anonymously as possible. He did not wish to communicate with *anyone* he knew back at Ocala. The tedious trip covered several thousand miles, took at least two weeks to complete, and was extremely exhausting; however, his relief at leaving his past behind him more than compensated for his weariness and discomfort. He stopped nightly at major cities along the way, grabbing as much rest as possible. He particularly delighted in the scenery as his travels took him out west. The broad horizons he experienced were a welcome relief from the endless, smothering Florida forests and greenery he had left behind.

Completely worn out, he eventually stumbled into his home, into his parents' and siblings' embrace. He was free at last … at least temporarily. He planned to lay low for as long as he could. His family listened to his tragic story and patiently comforted him as best they could. They empathized with his suffering and expressed their deep outrage at the manner in which he had been treated. To them, this was completely unfair.

After the remarkable meeting, Alistair had invited Alex to his office to discuss everything that occurred.

"Good God," said Alistair. "I never ever expected that to happen and with Roy in particular."

Alex responded quietly, "I don't think people appreciate how much damage they do to each other. Roy always appeared quiet and cheerful, but his promotion denial must have triggered another side of him entirely."

"It certainly appears that way," answered Alistair. "I never suspected he had such a dark side, but Ocala can certainly bring that out in you."

"People only look out for themselves and don't give a damn about the welfare of others. Appalling, to say the least."

The two friends commiserated with each other for some time, regretting the harm this report might do to the department's future. Scandals had, of course, occurred at other campuses but never to this extent or subject to such publicity. They wondered about the administration's reactions. The ultimate irony was that a denied tenure case might result in many of the department's faculty eventually losing their own permanent appointments in the future.

Alistair's macabre sense of humor eventually emerged as he said, "I heard we might do some downsizing but certainly not like this!"

Alex managed a wry smile. "After the recent scandal in the chair's office, we might all possibly be punished."

"This place damages people without their realizing it," responded Alistair.

The two friends discussed the report for a short time longer, grateful they had not appeared in it, then left the building to return home.

The dean reviewed Roy's investigative report with shock and concern. He forwarded a copy to the president who feared the increasingly negative publicity might damage Ocala's rising national rankings—Walter's major obsession. The dean appointed an evaluation committee with the interim department chair as its head. Many meetings followed, with an interim report provided to the dean after approximately a month. In the meantime, the accused sociology faculty were informed they were being investigated but should continue their academic duties for the present.

As is typical, the media had a field day with the news, spreading it as far as possible. They interviewed university officials and affected faculty, as well as former and current sociology majors. Alistair and Alex were disgusted and remained out of the spotlight completely. The unaccused also opted to remain silent and went about their normal activities as best they could. Some sociology courses were now unstaffed, and the interim chair reviewed these, cancelling some and refunding tuition to those affected.

The next time Alistair was on campus after Roy's investigation had been published, a student accosted him, complaining that some of her classes were not currently being taught. She blurted out, "They never let you forget you're at Ocala State!"

Alistair convulsed with laughter, agreed with her completely, and used this as a punchline whenever he was frustrated from then on.

No sooner had the situation calmed down somewhat than the protests commenced. Students at all levels complained about alleged sociology faculty behavior, while the union, encouraged and supported by Allen, demanded legal and financial support for all those accused. Lack of classroom instructors to complete a number of sociology courses, both graduate and undergraduate, only aggravated the situation. Choruses and signs demanding "Transparency Now!" and "Support Accused Faculty!" and "Protect Student Academic Needs!" were evident throughout the campus.

Several days later, the interim chair, dean, provost, and president huddled together to consider their options. They met for several days to thrash out plans to address current and future university needs. Major concern for student academic welfare was emphasized immediately and throughout the next several months as summer approached.

The sociology department held a meeting with all involved Administrators to air their concerns and address their needs. Major concern was expressed throughout the campus as well as the Board of Trustees. However, most participants were completely unaware of the upper-level administration's plans to close down the unit, support the unaccused faculty for a further six months, and try to relocate them to other campuses or facilitate their early retirement. Only the dean, provost, and president had discussed this possibility. Since this was not the first academic unit to be shut down on campus, this option appeared both attractive and feasible to them, offering major budgetary relief.

The Department's Fate

AFTER SEVERAL WEEKS, the dean felt uncomfortable keeping the plans to shut down the department confidential and gave the interim chair permission to announce it to the faculty. The news spread like wildfire, and protests ramped up with a vengeance.

Even Alistair felt this was completely outrageous. "Haven't we and others suffered enough?" he complained to Alex. "A significant number of colleagues have been accused, but they want to destroy the *whole* department?"

His bitterness was particularly aggravated by having given up everything in Scotland to establish roots at Ocala and serve the community, students, and university. To think he might still be in his homeland, in his sixties, moving toward the final stages of a successful career. He found restraining himself to be very difficult, almost impossible. "Can you imagine what I have now lost in career opportunities? I might have been better off had I remained in Scotland, despite fewer career opportunities there!"

"I'm afraid that no one cares, no matter what you have suffered," Alex responded.

"That's what makes it even more outrageous," concluded Alistair.

Noisy protests continued outside the department and Hambrook Building, involving students, faculty, and union organizers. Few people were able to enter or pursue their work for days on end. While Administrators attempted to negotiate a constructive resolution, they were met with continuous resistance. Community leaders also became concerned by the poor image this bestowed on the city and region as a whole, detracting from Ocala's image and regular recruiting efforts.

Finally, upper-level management tired of this interference with daily activities and considered options to bring the protests to an end. One of these was to designate a "zone of free speech," confining all protests to one area of campus. Some thought this might work; however, it was met with screams of "no freedom of speech," "it's unconstitutional," and "smacks of a dictatorship." Some Administrators were appalled by the intemperate behavior and demands of the protesters. The campus had become filled with the sounds of angry demands rather than an environment in which to think, debate, or learn.

The dean of faculty, an older professor close to retirement, was heard to comment, "Don't mind them; they're just *doing* their sociology!"

When Alistair heard this, he roared with laughter, commenting, "That sums it up perfectly!" His own anger did not subside, but he was forced to calm down the best he could. His imagination, however, kept working overtime.

Discussions of future plans continued for weeks and months as the department struggled to restore and maintain what remained of its teaching schedule. The union was also heavily involved in ongoing negotiations with the administration, but little progress was made.

Alistair feared the worst. His colleagues felt increasingly insecure regarding their future careers and planned to explore the job market that offered little reason for optimism. This placed a "cloud of doom" over everyone's head that appeared endless. Little enthusiasm remained for teaching, research, or writing. Everything seemed to stumble along with no meaningful end in sight. Furthermore, the department failed to develop internal consensus regarding future planning and helpful adaptations to the emergency, revealing its usual fault lines around faculty networks. The Mafia and Insiders were particularly vocal, as always. The lack of clear communication between the department and administration only made matters worse. The Insiders felt outraged by this unanticipated destructive action. As usual, the Vulnerable remained silent, not knowing what action to take regarding their fate. Many faculty became seriously depressed and rarely appeared in their offices. The Supporters were particularly disturbed by these developments, viewing them as unnecessarily destructive and damaging to Ocala's general reputation.

Eventually, the administration finally decided to hold a news conference to announce their decision. The president, provost, dean, and interim chair appeared together outside the main administration building.

After greeting everyone, President Jefferies spoke. "Thank all of you for coming to address this disturbing situation. I can only appreciate all the anger and difficulties many of you have experienced due to this investigation.

"The remaining faculty and students impacted by these accusations all have my deepest concern. Ocala is doing everything in its power to support their needs and facilitate their ongoing academic progress through the end of the semester.

"The department has clearly taken a major hit, and I strongly feel, along with other Administrators, that it will be extremely difficult, if not impossible, at this time to restore sociology to its previous condition."

He concluded by indicating they had agreed to begin a gradual downsizing of the academic unit until it was completely disbanded. Remaining faculty were to be retained at full salary for at least the next six months while efforts were made to transfer the innocent to available interdisciplinary programs, other departments in the town or state, or process them for early retirement where desired. Staff should expect to be treated in similar fashion as well as graduate students on assistantships or fellowships. The president added that he understood this was a radical proposal affecting everyone in the department and all students in the classes.

Several of Alistair's colleagues gasped in horror at this terminal news, complaining loudly at their "outrageous treatment." Alistair rolled his eyes in exasperation.

The provost then stepped forward to provide more details of these steps, emphasizing the extent to which all those affected were to be treated "with maximum consideration and respect." While not welcoming this action, the dean indicated his further concern and efforts to ensure that no one would be abandoned but fully transferred into other positions or retirement if they so decided. Those who wished to leave the campus immediately would also be accommodated. The interim chair regretted these steps even more so and also pledged to help everyone concerned with every resource available to him.

The meeting was then opened to questions. Many sociology faculty, particularly the Mafia, disputed the necessity for such dire steps. Others, such as the Supporters, asked "Why now?" And yet more, particularly the Radicals, expressed outrage at this destructive treatment of tenured, and in some cases, senior faculty who had committed their whole careers to Ocala. They began to discuss possibly lobbying the state legislature for assistance and conducting sit-ins. Their desire to protest this perceived injustice was overwhelming.

In the end, the president stated his feelings that full restoration of the department was too costly and unrealistic at this point in the university's development, and that this proposal, while unfortunate, served everyone's interest best.

Reporters also asked how this seemingly destructive plan might affect Ocala's reputation. The president replied, "While unfortunate, we feel our rankings and upward trend will not be heavily impacted by the loss of a sociology department."

Alistair had to smile wryly at this cynical but accurate observation.

The meeting closed, and the audience began to disperse.

These announcements further fueled ongoing controversy and objections. Faculty, students, and union officials organized a major protest that swamped roads and buildings throughout the campus, interfering with all major activities. The notion of "free speech zones" was totally ignored as people demonstrated wherever they wished. The campus police remained at a distance, refusing to provoke further negativity. These disturbances continued for several days before dying down and, eventually, disappearing completely. The media became heavily involved, portraying the situation as an "extreme crisis" threatening to destroy academic freedom and bring down the current administration. Of course, nothing of the kind had occurred.

Meanwhile, Alistair was holed up in his apartment, where he had remained for several days. The eventual demise of the sociology department had come as no particular surprise; after all, not long before, the president and provost had attempted to close down another social science department, based largely on its tumultuous faculty behavior. The arbitrator, however, had reversed the decision, and the department in question was slowly being restored. Nevertheless, Alistair found the present situation entirely unacceptable; it amounted to "kicking the victim when they were down." The sociology department had been seriously damaged through no fault of at least a few of its faculty.

He invited Alex over for a few drinks, and they considered the disaster in some detail. Alex had opted for early retirement but deeply resented the necessity to do so.

"This place has a long-term reputation for not giving a damn, taking the easy way out, always making everything about the money," Alex said.

Alistair responded, "Yes, but in this case, it's clearly a matter of punishing the victim who is largely innocent."

"But that doesn't matter. They don't even recognize the situation for what it is; only their own needs count."

"This is egregious and entirely unacceptable. I intend to do something about it."

"Oh, really? What exactly?" asked Alex.

"I have to give it some more thought but already have some ideas in mind. More later!"

They enjoyed a few more drinks, and then Alex left for home.

Alistair sat back in his easy chair and tried to organize his thoughts. His career had been destroyed unnecessarily through no fault of his own. Currently in his sixties, finding another position might be very difficult if not impossible, unless he was prepared to take anything available that was out there. He had left his homeland permanently, committing himself to a future at Ocala without reservation; he had learned the hard way, however, that Ocala was not committed to *him*. Had he failed to achieve tenure, he would have accepted the outcome and left willingly. Clearly, this was not the case.

He could now commiserate with Roy, thinking, *Nobody cares. The system is politicized and unfair, and the outcome despicable.* No doubt, things had always been this way and always would be. So what were his options?

He planned to take his payout and leave as soon as possible. However, why should the system that spawned this harmful outcome be permitted to continue unscathed? *That* was unfair. *Mediocrity only begets mediocrity.* He had experienced this firsthand for many decades at Third Rate U. He contemplated what Roy had done and what *he* might accomplish through nontraditional means.

He was aware he was becoming "radicalized" but felt he had been forced in this direction and allowed himself to wander down this alleyway and see where it might lead. Resentment offered few remedies—except, perhaps, revenge. What kinds worked for him? A number of destructive methods offered themselves; homicide, violent attacks, fraud, theft, and bombing represented but a few but were too violent to be considered seriously. On the other hand, the error would be to remain passive and accepting, allowing, the "Beast" to continue its uncaring, irresponsible, dysfunctional, and destructive ways unscathed.

At this point, he decided to finish his drink, eat dinner, and "sleep on it," allowing his subconscious mind to contemplate further "solutions." He slept fitfully, his dreams dark and difficult to interpret. His mind wandered in numerous directions, eventually waking him early the next day. He wished he could discuss his intentions with his wife but obviously couldn't in order to maintain his secrecy. He knew she was always concerned for his welfare, though she would understand his extreme frustrations. He wondered if she might have tempered his devastating plans for Hambrook.

Alistair's Plan

ALISTAIR STARTED TO WORK ON his "plan" at the start of the next decade. He researched possible actions and exit strategies. His major priority involved covering all his tracks and making his escape as efficient as possible. He spent hours debating the ethics of the destructive action he was pondering: Was it warranted, and did it serve any good purpose? Was it worth the risk and possible damage to his admirable wife and children who had patiently suffered his outbursts and constant venting on many occasions? How might it impact the rest of his life? Even if he were successful in getting away with the crime, how might he feel afterward, and could he handle the possible guilt and psychological damage to himself?

Such questions were balanced against the injury Ocala State and some of his colleagues had wrought on fellow faculty, seriously aggravated by not "giving a damn." They were blind to their own inhumanity and mediocre policies. The degree to which their self-interest overwhelmed any concern for the welfare of others disgusted him the most. Certainly, academic standards and integrity were important, but so was the humane treatment of all concerned. The academic world was possibly the most hypocritical and unkind of all, despite its pretensions. All the destructive forces of the past that had been leading up to this point had now reached their zenith, and the volcano was about to blow.

Keeping his destructive schemes completely to himself—revealing them neither to Alex nor his family—was clearly vital. As he began his research, he was amazed to find so much useful information on the internet. He planned slowly and carefully, not rushing any step. Visiting Ocala's Human Resources office to process his resignation, early retirement payout, and related paperwork was his first step. To ensure secrecy, he decided not to discuss his decision to leave, neither with his dean nor interim chair. Alex was to be informed later—after Alistair had left. Alistair's wife and children assumed this was all simply part of his final plan to leave Ocala and retire in Scotland. They could be enlightened later.

He required untraceable transportation to the airport. He purchased the plane tickets in cash, disguised in a wig and beard. The scheme concluded with stealing—borrowing—a student's car on campus the night before the event. Virtually all of his remaining belongings were sold at several garage sales over a number of weekends. Keeping calm and silent, particularly in his conversations with Alex and his wife, was very difficult. He was sorely tempted to reveal his intentions ahead of time but managed to keep silent. If his "mission" were to succeed, total silence and stealth were vital.

He managed to obtain a detailed architectural blueprint of Hambrook, including all its internal electrical and plumbing details. He discovered the water system was centralized in a major reservoir on the roof. Like many campus facilities, the building had few updates and still contained fire hoses housed in glass cases on each floor. At this, he smiled, and his imagination began to work overtime. He commenced to explore plumbing and engineering plans on the internet. Fortunately, as an undergraduate in Scotland, he had completed a year as an engineering student so had some relevant background in the field.

He knew *exactly* what he was going to do.

His aim was to connect Hambrook's sewage system with its roof water reservoir and then flood the building with this putrid mixture, using the fire hoses on each floor. He needed to connect the major sewage downflow pipe to the reservoir, using both a pump and filter to ensure only liquids entered the reservoir, without overflowing the system, thereby bringing its "revision" to anyone's notice. He began to plan obtaining the required supplies and suitable plumbing to enable this "detour" without attracting attention.

Given the building's security arrangements, it took him about a week to obtain the necessary building plans. He checked what was available on the internet as well as Ocala's planning department; both sources were helpful. He worked out how to gain internal access to the roof's reservoir without being discovered, lower the extra pipes to ground level, connect them to the basement sewage system, and install the pump and filter next to the storage tank. He also installed a float in the tank to cut off the sewage flow and pump when the tank was full, ensuring a continuous flow.

He worked on these tasks toward the end of each day at dusk when there were few students, workers, or others around. He wore plumbing overalls, a cap, and mask, keeping all materials in a scruffy van he had discovered—apparently abandoned by students given its grubby debris of smelly backpacks, empty beer cans, mucky notebooks, and worn textbooks. He used this vehicle as camouflage for his "plumbing" activities. Wearing gloves at all times to avoid direct contact with the vehicle, he managed to get it started and used it to carry his flooding supplies to Hambrook. He planned to abandon it later, after it had served its purpose.

He sat back and pondered his situation in depth. Understandably, he continued to wonder if he had reached the right decision. Despite serious attempts to avoid collateral damage, his intended action was extreme and went totally against his traditional values. Destructive force was rarely a solution to anything and tended to provoke irrational responses. However, no one at Ocala had ever appeared to wake up to see what was really going on, forever maintaining their state of delusional denial.

Visiting the department not long after the announcement of the department's demise, he found what remained to be in a state of almost complete disarray with hardly any classes operating effectively, taught by the few faculty who chose to help out remaining students by staying on to "the bitter end." The unnecessary destruction was appalling but reflected the way Ocala normally conducted business. *What a mess!* he thought and left Hambrook as quickly as possible.

Time passed slowly as a few weeks crept by. Alistair planned his future activities and goals upon his return to Scotland, intending to keep a low profile and remain as remote as possible. His family was packed off to Scotland a few weeks later. They had rented a small cottage outside Aberdeen where he planned to join them all later. He was sorry to see them go and regretted not being able to reveal his plans to them.

In the meantime, he emptied out his office, gave away most of his books, completed his course grades, shredded remaining papers, and moved out, leaving a travel poster of Tahiti on the wall. Would they ever notice he had left? Probably not.

He spent some of his remaining time with Alex, who knew he was retiring but had no idea of his destructive plan. They reminisced about the past, particularly the most peculiar recent events at Ocala, and looked forward to retirement but wondered how they might adjust. They parted after an enjoyable evening, and Alex returned to his apartment.

Alistair planned his final visit to Hambrook, preparing the battered van and its contents. The few remaining items in his apartment were sold off, leaving a bed and chair to be picked up after he left town. All his bank funds were withdrawn in cash to accompany him on his trip to Scotland. While bulky, he designed several money belts to fit around his waist to hold the currency, hoping they would enable him to pass through customs effectively. A neighbor bought his truck and would pick it up after he left town, so Alistair could use it in the meantime. After completing all these tasks, he relaxed in his last remaining chair, called his family to check on their condition, and enjoyed several drinks before turning in for the night.

The Dirty Deed

THE DAY FINALLY ARRIVED, waking Alistair with a start after a restless night with little sleep. All his bags for the trip were packed carefully, and he made some breakfast. The last day was bound to drag; to help, he had planned a final trip to the nearest beach. He packed a light lunch and took off in his truck.

The weather was temperate and very pleasant. He enjoyed taking walks along the beach but did not relish sunbathing; it bored him. After a comfortable trip, he arrived at the attractive resort. The sand was white, the sky blue, and the sea a beautiful green. A small crowd was tanning, surfing, and enjoying picnics. Soaking it all in, he knew he would miss this kind of ambience in the freezing mist and snow of Scotland. While he regretted having to leave, he knew his time was up, and he needed to depart anyway once the flooding commenced.

Leaving the beach midafternoon, he arrived home around 5 p.m. After a light supper, he started his final preparations for the "big event." He dressed in dark clothes, then relaxed. Once it was dark, he started looking for a car near campus he could take to travel to the airport and leave there when he left. He found an older model that was easy to hotwire—a skill he had acquired in his youth when he had dabbled in mild delinquency—and parked it near his apartment.

Resting until around midnight, he prepared to leave at approximately 3 a.m., a time that should minimize collateral damage. He hooked the van to his truck and slowly pulled out of the parking lot, arriving outside the Hambrook entrance at 3:30 a.m.

The night was cloudless, the sky brilliant with stars. After detaching the van, he drove his truck about a mile away. As usual, campus security was essentially nonexistent. He looked through the main entrance and did not see anyone. He thought he might have seen a light still on in the dean's office. He smiled grimly; Ron had treated him very poorly on several occasions, so what did he care? *Let him get what's coming to him. Certainly, no loss there.*

Having ensured his unnoticed arrival at Hambrook, Alistair prepared to start the sewage pump to fill the water reservoir. Staring intently at the building's tall silhouette, he proceeded. After several minutes, the water reservoir appeared infused with sewage as indicated by a wireless gauge he had installed. At that point, he rode the elevator to the top floor and turned each fire hose full force on every floor in turn, checking to ensure they were all contaminated with sewage.

The smell began to pervade the inside of the building, with resulting gas flowing to the exterior. Since all windows were sealed, the pollution would be complete and continuous as all the pump and cutoff switches were automatic. He checked to make certain each hose was successfully flowing, fully flooding each floor and its offices, ruining all their contents. Soon, the building would become a toxic mess and poisonous threat to all around.

The Leaning Tower

ALISTAIR LOOKED BACK AT HAMBROOK. The putrid gas starting to surround the building gave it a funereal air. The scene reminded him of a Viking cremation but without the honor. It was spectacular; against an intense blue backdrop of shining stars, the crippled tower appeared as a dark silhouette surrounded by a poisonous mist and purple-colored ambience. This view of destructive chaos was stunning. Ocala State would never be the same again, forever marked by this indelible stain of shame.

"Take that, you unthinking morons!" he shouted, shaking his fist at the sky. "Impossible to ignore such a stinking message!" Hambrook was now *Hambroke*. He chuckled at the joke and felt a rush of cathartic emotion flood his body and mind—free at last!

"I'm out of here!" he roared. He had to move quickly. Since his pollution system was self-monitored and continuous, the resulting flooding rapidly damaged the building's aging, crumbling foundation that was now surrounded by expanding sinkholes, and Hambrook began to lean. The site was now a major environmental and health risk. He was confident the structure could not be saved and required complete destruction, including all its occupants' property and data. This pleased him greatly. The bright sky silhouetted the putrid mist surrounding Hambrook.

A few passersby noticed the emerging fumes and building's slight tilt, and approached the main entrance slowly. The surrounding gaseous fumes, however, discouraged their going further, and many of them left to obtain help. Alistair was later pleased to learn that the whole building was indeed ruined, including faculty offices and their contents. He had accomplished a thoroughly terminal job. The surviving edifice would inevitably be condemned and destroyed entirely. Removal of the now endemic toxic waste required long-term effort and major expense. Alistair had definitely "left his mark!" Shortly after removing all his own possessions from campus, he warned Alex to evacuate his own office well in advance—a task the latter relished, similarly leaving a colorful island travel poster on his wall.

Not wishing to alert the police, Alistair drove his truck carefully back to his apartment. Wearing gloves, he threw his luggage into the "borrowed" car and drove calmly toward the airport. It being 4:30 a.m., he had plenty of time to catch his flight. When he reached the airport parking lot, he chose a space out of the usual line of sight and parked, switching off his lights. While he heard ambulance, police, and fire truck sirens at a distance, he felt he was in an oasis of quiet peace. His job was done, well done, and he could rest for now.

Feelings of serenity and calm washed over him as he rested. He sat and watched the dawn arrive, bringing with it silver then red light, accompanied by a slightly pink glow. He was absorbed into the utter beauty of the moment, temporarily minimizing the dirt and smell of the past night's activities. And then he changed his clothes.

A couple of hours later, he locked the car, grabbed his bag, and headed for the airport's front entrance. As he went in, he removed his plastic gloves, which he flushed down a toilet in the airport, making certain they completely disappeared.

Alistair's Exit

FEW PASSENGERS WERE VISIBLE in the building. He sat in front of the main entrance to security processing and patiently waited until the time was closer to his flight. He was checked through easily and proceeded to take a seat close to his flight's departure gate. This early in the morning meant a largely empty plane, and he looked forward to greater comfort than usual. He sat with his eyes and head down, reading a paperback novel. He had decided to take another look at Orwell's *1984*—amusingly relevant in light of recent events. Approximately thirty minutes later, he boarded and was shortly on his way to Chicago to make his connecting flight.

He had more than ample leg and head room, enabling him to take a short nap after his long and strenuous night. Not long after, coffee and a light breakfast were served, much to his relief since he had not eaten in some time. He ignored the passengers around him since he wanted to maintain his anonymity as much as possible. Eventually, copies of local newspapers were circulated, but it was too early to expect reports of Hambrook's demise—those would come later. The flight was comfortable, although bumpy at times. He kept to himself and read his book.

Landing at O'Hare was smooth, and once in the airport, he positioned himself well out of public sight and away from his next departure lounge. He bought a newspaper to check on the "main event" and found the report featured on the front page, showing a completely ruined aftermath. Some people, including several night staff and the dean, appeared temporarily unaccounted for, but there did not appear to be any confirmed fatalities. The buildings on either side had also been infused but to a lesser extent. Law enforcement officials were tight-lipped about their investigation, although they indicated they were doubtful this was a terrorist attack. The president indicated his horror at the damage and missing staff, emphasizing that they planned to clean up and rebuild in the near future. In the meantime, they attempted to hold classes in other buildings around campus. Alistair smiled wryly; they were as clueless and ineffective as usual. He planned to contact Alex after he arrived back in Scotland. At this stage, he felt relatively safe.

The afternoon went by slowly, and he eventually approached his departure gate for the direct flight to Glasgow. A few passengers were already seated in the lounge. He waited across the room in a chair near the window, read his book, and waited for boarding to begin. Eventually, he boarded and took his seat near the back of the plane where he settled in for further reading. The flight was far from full, and fortunately, he had several seats to himself. He enjoyed his dinner, as well as a mildly amusing movie, and slept soundly.

Later, he awoke to find signs of the rising dawn as they approached the outskirts of Glasgow. He experienced no problems moving through customs, much to his relief given all his money belts, and moved out into the main terminal. There he was very pleased to find his wife and two daughters, Mary and Kate, to greet him and was welcomed enthusiastically. They still remained unaware of his mission, which he intended to reveal to his spouse later. They gathered what little baggage he had, and boarded a rental van for the trip to Aberdeen.

The early morning traffic was picking up as they drove around Glasgow's outskirts and headed to their destination. The drive took several hours, in which everyone discussed their recent activities and enjoyment of their return to Scotland.

Alistair settled into his new role as retiree, relaxing and enjoying the beautiful countryside that passed by the van's windows. After a while, the outline of Aberdeen appeared on the horizon. They navigated slowly through the town to the outer suburbs, arriving at a small cottage near unoccupied land. This pleased Alistair since he wanted to have an escape route handy should he need one. He settled in with the small amount of luggage he had brought and relaxed with his family. They thoroughly enjoyed their reunion until it was time for his young adult children to retire for the night.

That evening, he informed his wife of what had occurred; she was immediately shocked and greatly concerned for his security. "What on earth persuaded you to undertake such a destructive course of action?" she asked.

He readily responded, "They treated me so badly and destroyed my career in such a degrading fashion. It was the least I could do!"

"Yes, but aren't you in imminent danger of arrest, even over here?"

"I understand your concern but have taken every possible precaution to protect my anonymity."

"Okay, then, assuming you have been adequately careful, while deeply uneasy, I can perhaps live with the results. The situation troubles me very deeply, though. I greatly hope it doesn't damage all of us."

After his reassurance, she began to relax, and they enjoyed a peaceful night together.

The next day, he settled into his new quarters, arranging his scant possessions, and examining what the cottage had to offer. While small, it was comfortable enough and accommodated them all easily. The girls would easily find nearby colleges or universities to resume their education. They both had developed strong academic records and clear professional career goals. Fortunately, the small house was isolated at the end of a long driveway, situated on a large parcel of land. They were all protected from prying eyes and grateful for it.

No longer at Ocala, Alistair could relax completely and considered the memoirs he planned to write, perhaps as fiction. He thought back on his destruction of Hambrook, anonymous escape, flights home, and trip to his new residence. Already, the excitement of recent events was largely behind him, and he started to enjoy his new privacy and freedom. He resisted appearing in town, keeping to the local village and its shops where he was largely unknown. People were largely friendly, accepting, and did not pry into each other's affairs. He found this refreshing and a relief after his recent life in the US, with its artificial joviality and empty friendliness.

A couple of days later, he called Alex to let him know how matters were progressing. They discussed Hambrook's recent fate. Obviously, Alistair could not reveal his part on the phone but described his new location and invited Alex over for a visit and short holiday. Alex readily agreed and planned his trip to occur in the next couple of months.

At that time, Alistair greeted his friend at the Glasgow Airport, and they talked continuously during the trip back to Aberdeen, focusing on their past at Ocala, recent events, and the way in which they had both been mistreated.

Alex was utterly amazed when he discovered Alistair's part in Hambrook's demise. "Congratulations on your bravery and skill, but aren't you concerned you might eventually be caught?"

Alistair responded, "I clearly appreciated the risk when I conceived the idea but am prepared to face the 'music' if and when I have to, given how ridiculous and blind Ocala State has become, and the damage it has wrought on so many good people."

Alex concurred, emphasizing, "I will do everything possible to protect your privacy."

Given his firsthand experience, Alex described what remained of the ruins left behind and the inhibiting effects on the social science departments on campus for a long time to come.

While there had been some resettling and temporary accommodations elsewhere, the college was seriously crippled, as was its dean; Ron had apparently stayed at his office very late to meet some vital deadlines and became seriously ill after having to wade through huge amounts of sewage to escape the building. His immunity was now at an all-time low.

Alistair smiled with satisfaction; for now, he had triumphed!

PART FOUR: BACK AT OCALA

BACK AT OCALA, the atmosphere remained polluted by overwhelming amounts of toxic gas, seriously hindering major cleanup efforts. The administration had campus law enforcement look into the pollution; however, given their ineptitude, they quickly turned to the FBI and State Department of Law Enforcement as the major investigators. Conspiracy theories abounded, with several new ones invented on a daily basis. Students and faculty made weak attempts to protest the emergency; these were ignored and viewed as unwelcome and irrelevant detractions. Many social science courses eventually had to be canceled for lack of facilities and instructors willing to continue under such toxic conditions. Some faculty started to suspect each other, somewhat akin to the McCarthy Era: *Could they? Might they? Why would they? Do they really think this helps? Why did this have to happen to us? What did we do to deserve such a fate? How does this help anything?* As usual, narcissistic egos were in overdrive, blaming others and whining over their own temporary losses.

Eventually, most of the building was gutted, with the debris removed carefully to ensure environmental safety. Few approached the toxic site since it threatened the safety of anyone who came near it. Adjacent buildings had to be roped off, restricting admission and then only under restricted conditions. Agents started interviewing affected faculty, exploring any explanations they might entertain; not surprisingly they had little substantial to offer.

After a while, the stolen student car was discovered but contained no identifying evidence. The van was eventually discovered also but lacked any useful fingerprints or identifying marks. Lists of faculty who had left town recently were drawn up and checked; however, since Alistair had processed his retirement before leaving, his absence was not viewed as suspicious. The FBI also requested help from Interpol to check people who had recently entered other countries; fortunately, Alistair wasn't conspicuous due to his Scottish origins.

President Jefferies felt obliged to consult the state legislature for extra funding and emergency help to restore the campus to its previous state and protect the welfare of its students and faculty. Local politicians were eager to be as supportive as possible, particularly regarding rebuilding efforts; several million dollars were made available almost immediately and restoration plans put into action. Alistair followed all this development from afar, elaborated by further details provided by Alex.

What stood out as amazing, but not surprising, was the complete lack of questioning as to *why* such an event might occur. It was simpler to label it as "terrorism"' or a "crime" and prosecute it as such in the normal unthinking manner. Mediocrity, of course, is not only sloppy but also unthinking, grossly unaware of its surrounding environment and possible problems within it, causing people to act in extreme ways when confronted with "brick" or "cement" walls of uncaring resistance.

The Faculty Senate held several emergency meetings, during which they waffled endlessly, passed motions supporting affected faculty and their families and student welfare, and called for immediate investigations and funding to enable rebuilding efforts. They also recommended tuition refunds for courses that were ended by the pollution. Most of these were accorded unanimous approval and forwarded to the president. The campus remained heavily toxic with remaining toxic fumes and debris. The ambience reminded visitors of a largescale garbage dump.

After several weeks, with little progress occurring, the governor met with President Jefferies in search of an explanation. His approach was heated, opening with, "Walter, what is going on here with this situation? Anything? I see so little progress; I have to wonder if you really know what you are doing!"

Jefferies responded, "I'm sorry you see it that way, governor, but these situations are complicated and take time to address."

"How long does it have to take? Do you have any clue what you are doing and why this happened?"

"I believe so," said Jefferies as reassuringly as possible, adding, "You can't solve these kinds of situations overnight."

The governor responded, "While I appreciate the difficulties, it appears to me you should have made more progress by now."

The governor knew when he was beat and left, vowing to pressure the board of governors to remove and replace Jefferies as soon as he could. He thought to himself, *They don't call this place "Mediocre U" for nothing. I'm so relieved I completed my law degree elsewhere.*

PART FIVE: FREEDOM!

BACK IN ABERDEEN, Alistair and Alex were enjoying their evening drinks outside. Unfortunately, this was Alex's last day; he was about to leave on the morning flight out of Glasgow. They had enjoyed a very relaxing vacation together, visiting Glasgow's bookstores and magnificent art galleries endowed by wealthy benefactors. Alistair had visited the city as a young child during the 1950s, when much of it was unsightly and very unpleasant. Fortunately, some decades later, local millionaires had decided to support the city's renovation and establishment of museums and art collections. Consequently, the city gradually became a very attractive place to visit its impressive cultural facilities. They spent several days there, enjoying the sights as well as the many pubs available.

They discussed Alex's return to Ocala, something he dreaded. Alistair encouraged him to consider joining him in Scotland, and Alex indicated he intended to give the matter serious thought. They also discussed the positive consequences of Alistair's retirement; away from the daily stupidity and irrationality of academic life, he was miraculously at peace. It was almost as if he had started life over and was free to live as he wished—finally! His whole body had calmed down as he felt deeply relaxed.

Alistair emphasized, "Being so absorbed in Ocala, particularly its academic irrationality, low self-awareness, lack of attention to detail, delusional perspectives, and mediocrity, I was forced to struggle for air. It was only when I was able to step out of the sinkhole that I could actually see it for what it was: an airtight, toxic bubble of self-delusion, creating constant anxiety and self-doubt, reinforced by an environment full of 'true-believers.' No wonder I wanted to tear it down and destroy it. It represented a seductive delusion designed to draw in the young, rob them of self-confidence, and make them dependent on the system for approval and personal identity. I now feel completely emancipated from my previous servitude and cleansed of its poison. *Now*, I can actually *see*. Furthermore, I don't feel any real guilt over my actions."

Alex queried, "Why do you think that is?"

Alistair replied, "I think that in of the corrupt treatment we suffered at all levels at Ocala, destroying Hambrook was deeply cathartic. I now feel calm and completely revenged."

Alex responded, "I completely understand and agree with you. I now plan to return to Ocala to finalize my retirement arrangements and settle in Scotland as soon as possible. Being single will make this easy."

Alistair was extremely pleased, expressing how much he looked forward to Alex's return. They enjoyed their last evening together, drinking and reminiscing.

Early next morning, they traveled to Glasgow Airport, and Alistair wished his friend a safe and enjoyable trip home. He returned to Aberdeen in good spirits, but that very day, he received a call from an FBI agent, querying him about his early retirement and "coincidental" exit to Europe. Alistair responded as calmly and in as much detail as possible, obviously leaving out all his acts of destruction that occurred prior to his flight. The agent seemed satisfied with his answers, indicating they had checked his fingerprints against all the evidence and found nothing suspicious. However, the officer closed by saying he might call back later or ask Interpol to meet with Alistair in Glasgow if necessary.

Back in Florida, in an effort to trace the perpetrator, law enforcement was also examining parts of the building and its installed equipment. Alistair found this unsettling and started to think his days might be numbered. Nevertheless, despite the danger of arrest and extradition, he concluded that what he had done was completely worth it. He had struck back and made them think. Come what may, he had rebelled rather than submit to the Ocala Beast!

Nevertheless, the agent's call made him consider developing serious security precautions for himself and family. He examined various "escape routes" out of town, particularly those available close to his cottage. He also looked into the possibility of constructing an underground bunker or shelter on the property to protect them from capture if necessary. Further research, however, revealed this as too likely to expose him to local suspicion. He examined other options, including escape to islands near the area, possibly using a small aircraft. He looked into both and checked into the availability of local flying lessons and planes. While both appeared available, he concluded they might draw unnecessary attention to his recent arrival and decided to focus on other matters.

A few days later, an Interpol agent called the cottage and asked if he could visit, to which Alistair agreed. The interview was unsettling, but he answered all the agent's questions as fully as possible.

The visitor probed all Alistair's movements and actions prior to leaving Ocala, indicating, "The agency continues to be suspicious of your leaving Ocala permanently, as well as the US, so quickly."

"Given the destruction of Hambrook," Alistair said, "closing of the sociology department, and the end of my academic career, I was forced to retire and decided to settle back in my home country with my family."

The agent probed further. "What events exactly took place, causing you to not only leave Ocala but the country as well? Also, I need to check your personal records before I leave, please."

Alistair responded readily, providing him with full information regarding what had occurred and gave him copies of his personal documents. The agent thanked him and indicated these items might be very useful in Interpol's ongoing inquiry.

Alistair queried him regarding what the investigation had discovered and was told they were still looking into everything but had few leads.

"We are considering the possibility of some kind of dangerous gas leak or homegrown terrorism," the agent said.

Alistair's heart leaped inside him with relief at this news; it appeared he had successfully escaped discovery—at least for now. The agent thanked him and left.

Free at Last!

RECENT EVENTS, as well as the new millennium's successes, were cause for celebration. Alistair and his wife enjoyed a large bottle of the finest Scotch, during which two thoughts dominated Alistair's amused mind: *Tenure denied ensures others are fired!* and *A soiled department makes for a ruined building!* The irony overcame him, and he laughed uncontrollably. His long-term tension, anxiety, and stress were now completely cleansed; he could finally relax in peace. Noxious Ocala, Hambrook, and the department within it had all receded into dim memory. He could now move on with his life in peace.

Next morning, a brilliant red sunrise welcomed him to his new life. The destructive past had disappeared, and his escape was complete. Ocala had vanished completely from his life and mind. He sat back and smiled at his good fortune.

Heather commented, "You finally appear at rest."

"I am," Alistair replied, thankfully.

www.ingramcontent.com/pod-product-compliance
Lightning Source LLC
Chambersburg PA
CBHW021426200626
46814CB00015B/1540